Tales of the Modern Realms
By Jack Harvey

Tales of the Modern Realms

Contents

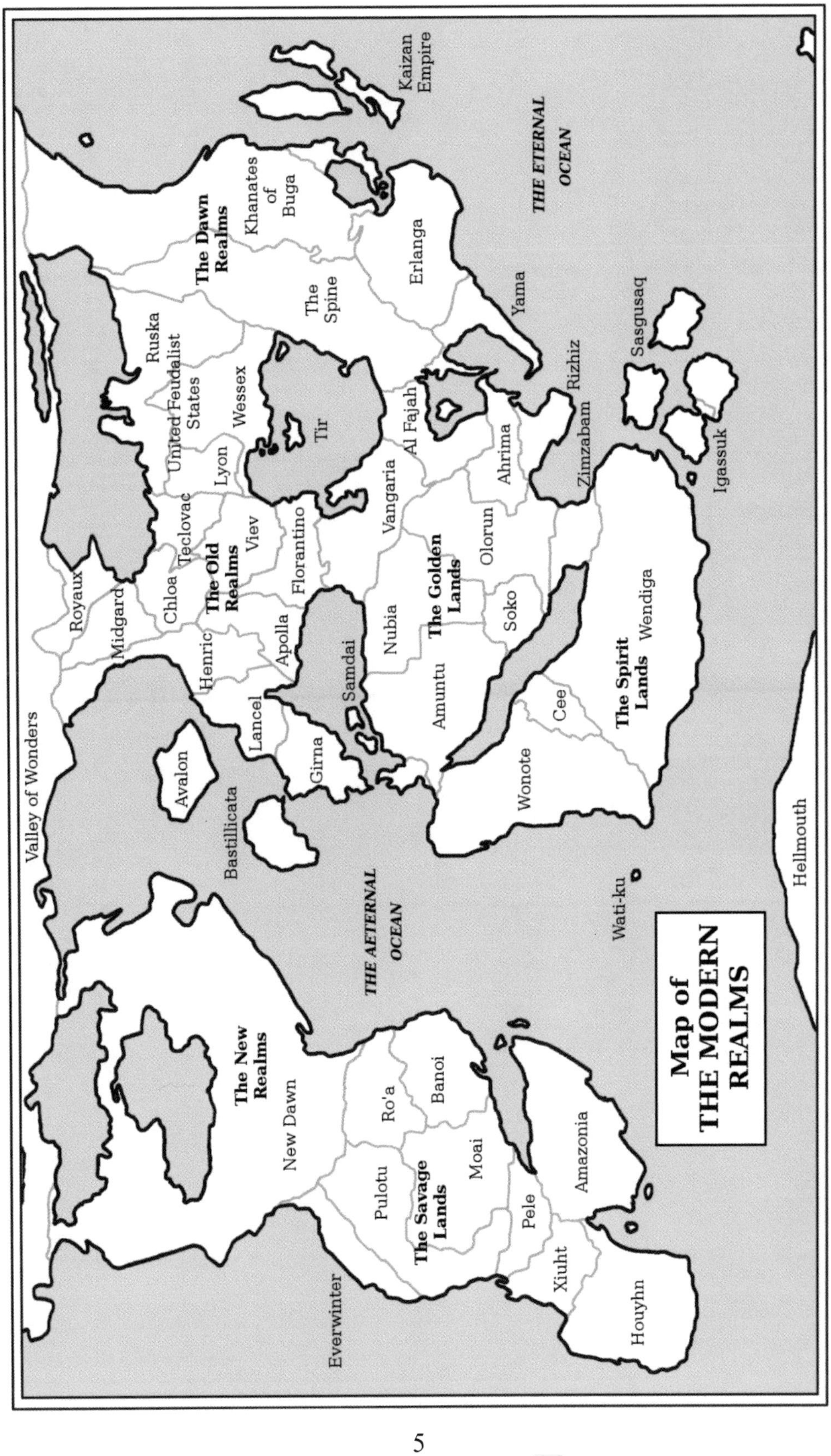
Map of
THE MODERN
REALMS
Kaizan Empire
THE ETERNAL OCEAN
The Dawn Realms
Khanates of Buga
Erlanga
The Spine
Yama
Sasgusaq
Ruska
United Feudalist States
Wessex
Tir
Al Fajah
Rizhiz
Lyon
Ahrima
Zimzabam
Igassuk
Teclovac
Viev
Vangaria
Florantino
The Old Realms
Olorun
The Golden Lands
Royaux
Chloa
Midgard
Nubia
Soko
Wendiga
Apolla
Henric
Samdai
Amuntu
The Spirit Lands
Cee
Lancel
Valley of Wonders
Girna
Avalon
Wonote
Bastillicata
THE AETERNAL OCEAN
Wati-ku
Hellmouth
The New Realms
New Dawn
Ro'a
Banoi
Moai
Pulotu
The Savage Lands
Amazonia
Pele
Xiuht
Everwinter
Houyhn

Tales of the Modern Realms
NEW · REGIME · PRESS · FICTION ·
NR
£0.46
Free!
DOUBLE TAP
A Percy Evangelyne
Story
By Jack Harvey
JH
2014

Modern Realms

Double Tap

A Percy Evangelyne Story

By Jack Harvey

Percy Evangelyne picked at his teeth in a vain attempt to dislodge a rogue piece of tobacco. It had been a while since he had been placed in the field. Oh, he had served his time in the past, proved his worth under pressure. Even so, he still worried that prolonged office work had left him rusty.

Percy shouldn't really have been here. He was officially attached to the codebreakers now, but the service was light on agents at the moment, and they needed one at short notice to deal with their little problem. Percy didn't really mind, he'd been hankering for some proper field work for ages. He would have just liked a bit of an advance for a job like this, that's all.

He looked at his pocket watch, cool gold against his green skin, and he scratched the carefully groomed branches that grew out of his scalp. Percy was an earth born human, that is to say his features take on the qualities of that particular element. His colleague, Aric Silver, who was now testing his patience, was a water born elf, and this was reflected in his blue skin.

Percy sighed, his mind filling with worried thoughts. He questioned the wisdom of pairing up two of the department's best elementally touched agents. Though ten percent of the population were elemental born, their talents were in high demand. Woodrow Henderson, head of the service, insisted they didn't have time to be pedantic. He was stubborn, as all dwarfs were.

Out of the smog of Hightower's streets he finally saw Aric approach. He was a tall and handsome elf, always wore a shirt unbuttoned once at the top, complemented by a pinstriped waistcoat. He'd been in the service longer than Percy had, but then again, elves did live much longer lives.

“Been chasing tail as usual?” Percy said, humour in his voice.

Aric didn't smile. "Another jibe like that and I'll shoot your bollocks off."

That probably meant that he had, and unsuccessfully at that. Despite him finding some of Aric's more unsavoury characteristics distasteful, the two were as good as friends. It had been a long time since they'd worked together.

"Well?" Percy asked, propping another cigarette between his lips.

"Takasugi Taro." Aric said, his cool smooth voice a contrast to the edge Percy felt he was walking. "He'd assumed the identity of a Kaizen businessman. We're not sure if he's been in contact with anyone in the service, but we do know he has been gathering intel for at least six months."

"The Kaizen Empire? Fuck. The way Woodrow was talking I thought we were dealing with the Feudalists."

Aric winced at the profanity. "The Feudalist Bloc may be Avalon's most immediate threat, but that doesn't mean we shouldn't take the Kaizens seriously, especially if the two decide to pally up."

"So that's it then?" Percy said with a grim finality. "Wetwork. No detention or interrogation, just pop pop pop. The old double tap?"

"What?" said Aric, confused at the mathematics of Percy's statement.

"Double tap," Percy repeated as he pulled out his pistol to check it was loaded and in working order. "Once in the body, once in the back of the head. Don't you remember your training?"

"I remember my training," Aric scoffed, as he pulled out his own antiquated broom handled pistol and checked it. "They just had two pops in my day. Why you youngsters have to be so theatrical I'll never know."

Percy shook his head. "An elf calling me theatrical. Urak's hammer, what are the realms coming to?"

They had begun to traverse the alley now, out onto the gaslit road. Percy smiled, Aric didn't look a day older than he did, but the elf had lived through The War of 3000 Mages, The Industrial Revolution, and a multitude of civil wars on the mainland. Percy was a baby to him.

“No need to question my ability Percy. It's you I'm worried about. Have you ever had to pull the trigger?” Aric said in a concerned, fatherly tone.

“Fortunately not, and personally I'd like to keep it that way.”

Aric raised an eyebrow. “You object to our little mission tonight?”

Percy tossed his cigarette to the floor. “I don't question orders. Doesn’t mean I have to like them.”

Aric smirked.

“That's why Woodrow wants you doing it.” Percy said. “Should be second nature, you used to go around beheading cyclopes single-handedly when you were in the Rangers back in the day, right?”

“Back in the day,” Aric grinned, “Not as commonly as you'd think.”

“And anyway, I suppose with this Takasugi Taro being Kaizen makes it all a little personal doesn't it? After what the empire did to your people during the purges?”

“Not my people,” Aric noted. He was referring to the still debated question that there was any common ancestry between Aric's elven people and the elves of the Kaizen islands. Some saw their plight as a common cause, though most, like Aric, felt they owed them very little.

They waited for the last of the traffic to dissipate before they crossed the road. Up ahead was the office that Takasugi Taro worked at, supposedly doing overtime. Their reports said that he was always the last to leave the building. It would be then that the grizzly business would take place.

“I hate this,” Percy said, watching Taro's silhouette flitter between the yellow light of the building's windows.

“Our's is not to question why Percy,” Aric said with confidence, and he heard the click as Aric thumbed back the hammer of his pistol. “You said as much yourself.”

Percy thought about that. Was this what he really wanted when he signed up all those years ago? He knew that if Taro didn't die tonight then he would be absconding by air tomorrow with untold secrets. The realms were already on the brink of war again, the last thing the service wanted was Avalon at a disadvantage. Yet he knew to grow accustomed to this business would signal the end of his empathy. He would become like Aric.

The lights of the office extinguished. Percy counted the seconds, holding his breath. On cue, their eyes moved from the window to the back door. Illuminated in the distance was the great statue of Urac, God of Order, looking down in judgement.

"Right then," said Percy, thumbing back the hammer of his own pistol. "Lets do this."

****

Another alley, another block of flats. It wouldn't be long until Taro noticed them following. It would have to be now.

"Just have to hope he doesn't have any spells up his sleeve," whispered Percy.

"There was nothing in his file," muttered Aric, who turned to make sure they weren't being followed. "Be seeing you in thirty." He nodded, then disappeared across the street.

It was now down to Percy to tail Taro. To keep an eye out for unexpected moves whilst Aric flanked him. It was standard wetwork procedure, to keep the target distracted so that he doesn't see his real killer coming.

Percy's mind was awash with doubts. Who was Taro? A kind man? A gentle man? Was he a killer himself? Did he have family? Children? Percy thought of his own two mothers, deceased now, and his mind quickly leaped to thoughts of his own mortality. Could Taro have a concealed weapon? An enchanted artefact? Maybe he did indeed know a spell or two, like Percy did.

Too late for doubts now. His brisk steps brought him closer, his breath in the cold air blowing back into his face. He could see Taro's short hair now. His stocky frame. He had to know, surely, that his time had come.

Hand on pistol, heart in mouth, Percy stared intensely at his target. The path where Aric and he would both intersect was mere inches away. Would Taro turn in confrontation? Try to run? Seconds now. Taro's head turned just slightly, Percy could only see his small broad nose, his eyes were in shadow.

Aric strolled into view, hand behind his back. Taro turned. Aric lunged, pistol raised, and Percy prepared for the crack of the gunshot.

Like lightning another figure came into view. A blur. They kicked Aric in the arm, which threw him into the alley's brick wall. Percy didn't have time to think. It was a trap. Taro turned, his own gun raised, and Percy whipped out his and they both fired blindly.

Percy felt the round bore through his thigh. Unlucky, it had hit the artery just south of the groin. A fatal wound. What was going on around him was just noise now. He was losing too much blood. Unlucky, so damned unlucky.

He pressed his hand to the wound, but that did little to stem the bleeding. His feet caved and the slippery wet ground greeted him about as well as one would expect. He fought to remain conscious. If he didn't get medical attention soon he'd be a gonner. Little hope on a covert operation, but Percy would never have lasted this long without his own tricks.

Early in his career he had been doing field work in the Wendinga forest, the largest confederation of the Spirit Lands, and seat of the high council of druids. As an earth born he had a natural talent for earth magic, but he was no druid. During his time there he had met Gendenwitha, an old druid master, wise of the art. Though she was not so old that she could not teach the young and impressionable Percy a thing or two. *Both in the bedroom and in the field*, Aric used to joke, missing the irony that he was centuries older than she.

"Percy felt the round boar through his thigh.
Unlucky, it had hit the artery just south of the groin.
A fatal wound. Unlucky, so damned unlucky."

It was the latter that was important to him now. Above all else the peoples of the Spirit Lands were healers. Healers of the land, healers of the self. Though Percy had always been far from grasping their ways, Gendenwitha had taught him a ritual that had kept him alive many a time, though the situation had never been as dire as this.

To be one with the land is to be one with one's self, Gendenwitha had said. *To control the self, one must become one with the land.*

To the Spirit Landers, who's society had a very ecological bent, this had meant hearing the wind between the trees, or seeing through the eyes of the hawk and the wolf. Yet Percy had come from a life of brick and iron. No hawks or wolves would be of help to him here. Though the Druid's often took inspiration from nature, it was becoming one with everything that gave earth magic it's true power.

Through blurred eyes Percy saw Aric in peril. This assailant was clearer now. She was female, a Kaizen like Taro. She fought like a brawler, no finesse here. The flurry of uncalculated blows against Aric were taking their toll, but, for the slender elf that he was, he was holding his own. No doubt his stubborn refusal to ever acknowledge a woman could fight like a man was proving a hindrance here though. Aric was a principled man after all.

His mind awake, Percy knew he had to act now. “To be one with the land is to be one with one's self. To control the self, one must become one with the land.” He drew a breath, blocked out the pain. He would have to become one with his land if he hoped to draw upon that natural earth magic. He needed a focus, something to ground himself to.

He thought of his adopted mothers. The lady and her bodyguard. They had taken him in, despite their age, despite their relationship, and to hell with what anyone else had thought. He thought of the freshly cooked biscuits of his youth. He felt the smooth pages of new books they always brought him every birthday. He remembered the warmth of their hugs on the day of his graduation.

He felt the pain of their passing far too early in his life. He remembered the love they had given him when his true father had cared so little. Left him at an orphanage not even old enough to say a word.

Percy felt joy, happiness, pain, regret, grief, relief and comfort. All the sins and virtues of his world. He was one with it. He was one with the land, just as Gendenwitha had taught him.

The rest was easy. Slow blood, mend flesh, renew life. Through the muffled sound of trading blows Percy felt the bleeding stop, his heart calmed and readied itself. The flesh around the wound knit itself together, the artery rejoined. Fragments of bullet ejected themselves. Then that was that, he was alive. Earth magic, the most complex, but mundane of magics.

Taking a few moments to centre himself, Percy had noticed that Aric and the woman had stopped fighting. She struggled, but Aric had restrained her against the wall, his pistol to her head.

The two were both bloodied, and she looked like she was just moments from breaking out of Aric's grip and giving him another beating.

Percy shook his head, looked at Taro's bullet riddled corpse. The old double tap? Yeah right. Yet still the worst was to come.

"Thought we'd lost you there Percy." Aric said, trying to hold the girl still.

"Old earth magic trick," he said dismissively, the mission taking precedence over any desired grandstanding. "Well what are you waiting for?"

"What?" asked Aric, shocked. "She's just a girl Percy, we can't just kill her."

He could see her clearer now. She wore a tight woman's blouse, sleeves rolled up to the elbows, and pinstriped trousers. Practical shoes. Her hair was tied up in a small knot bun, not uncommon for her people. She looked hardened, uncompromising.

"She's a girl that's just kicked your arse Aric."

Aric looked confused. "What happened to the man who could barely stand to consider the mission."

*"The two were both bloodied,
and she looked like she was just moments from
breaking out of Aric's grip and giving
him another beating."*

Percy had to ask himself the same thing. "I guess self preservation is a powerful motivator."

She shouted something in Kaizen at Aric, who in turn said something back, also in Kaizen.

"I didn't know you could speak the language?" said Percy, unconsciously trying to put off the morbid deed.

"You can't? I thought you were supposed to be a codebreaker?"

"I know the language to read, not to speak," he stated, as he limped forward. "Probably the opposite in your case. Look, she's a Kaizen agent. I don't like it either Aric but if Taro goes, so does she."

The two babbled something to each other again. It sounded as though Aric was trying to encourage her to trust them. Idiot was probably trying to negotiate, Percy thought.

Then something caught his eye. A red line running down the girl's arm.

"Aric wait. Turn her over, let me see her left arm."

Aric shoved her around. She seemed to have calmed a little now, struggled less. Aric still kept his gun trained to her forehead though. Percy looked at the elaborate tattoo that ran down her athletic and well toned arm. A dragon, surrounded by roses and thorns.

"Oh fuck, she's a Dracomon."

The Dracomon were a Kaizen criminal organization that had long ago originated as dragon slayers. Where most of Kaizen society had been associated with finesse and subterfuge, the Dracomon instead excelled in the art of brute force, both on the battlefield and off. It was rumoured that they still illegally hunted the now protected dragons, not for honour or gold, but for their blood that had now become common as a powerful narcotic.

Aric and the girl traded more words. For a moment Percy thought it was going to kick off again. Instead, both of them calmed down and Aric lowered his pistol.

"It's all been a terrible misunderstanding," Aric said with a little too much joy. "It seems that we've been working at cross purposes. She was also here to kill Taro. She thought we were here to protect him."

Percy felt relief, but hardly the relief that Aric did. Sure she wasn't a Kaizen agent, but she was part of a violent criminal organization. How did that make things better?

"Listen," said Aric diplomatically. "I'll take her back to the station house, see what she knows about Taro. You stick to the plan and dispose of the body.

"Take her back?" Percy said, shaking his head. "Aric she's a Dracomon. See those flames on her arm, they earn those for every enemy they kill." Percy looked at the girl through squinted eyes, trying to determine if she could understand what they were saying. He braced himself. "Who knows what she's learned from Taro? A criminal is just as dangerous as an enemy agent."

"What are you trying to say?" Aric's voice was part disgust and suspicion.

"You know what I'm trying to say. Aric" Percy spoke the words slowly to bestow meaning. *Kill her*, he thought. He wanted to mentally project that to Aric. She was part of a group that thought pulling someone's eyes out was a good way to negotiate territory. He couldn't possibly understand why Aric thought letting her away would be a good idea.

"No," Aric said. "I don't believe I do." He motioned to the girl and they began to walk away. "Stick to the plan and dispose of the body. Meet us at the station house when we're done."

Percy realised that he could do it now. With their backs turned. Pop pop pop. The old double tap. Aric could do little but complain once the deed was done. However, Percy remained frozen in place. Despite what he tried to tell himself, he couldn't really do it.

There had already been one too many deaths tonight.

****

Rain began to spatter Percy's shoulders. He looked to his feet. To any onlooker it was just a roll of carpet. Nothing sinister at all. People take carpets to the landfill all the time. Nothing suspicious about it. Not even at this time of night.

There was a hollow feeling in Percy. He looked down at what remained of Taro. An undignified end. Percy never thought of himself as a man without honour, yet even with his reservations stated he could see little honour in this.

His foot slowly pressed against the carpet and it rolled slowly across the grass, before toppling down into the deep brown pit. Just another piece of refuse.

Percy lit a cigarette and peered off into the night sky. He could see that statue of Urak again. It was turned away from him this time, looking more like a cold homeless man from this angle than a vengeful god of order. Not even the gods felt the need to sit in judgement over him on this one.

Percy exhaled slowly as the tobacco kick gave him a rise. Maybe he had been looking at this the wrong way. Maybe objecting to the bad wasn't the way to do good. Maybe instead he should be trying to do good in spite of the bad.

His heart skipped a beat. Maybe he didn't belong with the codebreakers after all. Maybe his place was here, right beside Aric in the field.

Percy threw his cigarette into the pit. The hollow feeling had gone, filled with something else. Something like duty.

****

Percy stopped off at a public toilet to clean up the blood on his trousers in order to avoid any awkward questions. Within minutes he was at the station house, an inconspicuous building listed as a solicitors.

He greeted the tired agent who was posted at the door. He was a man Percy didn't recognise, but then again he had been in the codebreakers for a while now. He asked if Aric had arrived with the girl.

"The cad is at it again," the man said through a smile. "Where'd he pick one up from this time?"

It took a moment for Percy to figure out the man was talking about the girl. He shrugged. "You know Aric," he said, brushing it off.

"I don't know why he bothers. With the vow and all."

Percy nodded, and headed to meet Aric upstairs. He twisted a worn brass knob on a rugged door.

"Well?" he asked.

"Her name is Ando Yoshiko. She says that her organization had been tracking Taro for quite some time. He'd been responsible for the deaths of several Dracomon superiors, and that he was to pay with his life for this slight."

"She sounds like a lovely girl."

"Don't be obtuse." Aric said, scowling. "Now that Taro's dead she herself can't exact the appropriate retribution. She says that to return to the Dracomon would be to return dishonoured. She's genuinely considering jumping ship."

"And you believe her?" Percy stated, amazed at Aric's perceived gullibility. "The Dracomon don't fuck around. If she'd been truly dishonoured she would have already killed herself." Percy looked around. "Where is she anyway?"

"She's just powdering her nose." Aric nodded towards the toilet. "I understand your reservations Percy but just think about what this could mean for the service."

"That's what this is all about is it Aric? Loyalty to the service?" Percy pulled out a cigarette and lit it up. "More like loyalty to your bedpost. I thought you were supposed to be celibate?"

"I am!" gasped Aric, shocked at such an accusation. "Not by choice, but I am." He began to undo the second button on his shirt. He was getting a little warm now after coming in from the cold. "That doesn't necessarily mean that a drink is off the cards."

"I knew it." Percy almost laughed but was too frustrated for that now. "I knew it wouldn't take two minutes for you to turn on that Aric Silver charm." Percy checked his gun.

"Percy, she's only a woman, she's harmless."

"Aric, she's a cold blooded killer! And even if she wasn't, I've seen the wonderful, terrible things women are capable of. She had you dead to rights, why can't you accept that?"

"She caught me off guard." Aric shrugged.

"She was stronger than you." Percy pointed aggressively at him.

Aric folded his arms.

"I respect that woman too much to know we can't let her get away alive."

Aric gave a brief laugh. "Not your call to make. I already sent the message to central, I'm awaiting their response now."

Percy and Aric looked gravely at each other. Their friendship was beginning to be pushed to it's limits.

"Aric, trust me."

"Give me one reason to." Aric pointed a finger at Percy. The tension in the air was palpable.

Percy didn't need to answer. Within a second the building shook, and they heard what sounded like a jack-hammer coming from the vicinity of the toilet.

The two agents ran to the door. Aric got there first, tried the handle. When it didn't work he give the door a couple of kicks, the third one bringing it down.

There was a craterous hole in the toilet wall, big enough to fit a person through, and no sign of Yoshiko. Painted on the wall in blood was a message in Kaizen. Aric ran to the breach, looking out for any sign of the girl. Percy was more taken by the message.

"No sign," Aric said. "What does it say?"

"I thought you knew Kaizen?" Percy replied.

"I never learned how to read it. You're the codebreaker, you figure it out."

Percy recognised the symbols from the Kaizen's unorthodox alphabet.

"Well, first symbol denotes an apology, sympathies. Second is dismissive. Personal dislike. Third symbol is masculine, that of the male gender."

Aric didn't seem to understand. He shook his head at Percy to indicate his confusion.

"Sorry, I'm not into guys," Percy said, smiling.

Aric's face turned into a moody frown, which quickly gave way to anger. He pulled out his pistol from it's holster and ran for the door. "Come on, she can't have gone far."

Percy wanted to laugh, "Oh, so now that a date is no longer on the cards Mr Silver doesn't care for her life any more, is that how it is?"

Aric, humiliated that he'd been taken for a ride, still understood how petty he was now being. He put his gun on the table, and the two men wandered over to the window.

"What do we do now?" Aric said, dejected.

"Hope she was telling the truth? Hope that she was only here to take care of Taro?" Percy slapped Aric on the shoulder. "Not a lot we can do now really, she's long gone."

"We're going to look like a pair of fools for this aren't we? I'm going to look like a fool."

"We'll leave it off the report," Percy smiled. "Tell the agent downstairs that a gas valve blew and took out the wall. Tell central the message was a miss-communication about Taro." All in all, he was relived that a difficult decision had been taken away from him.

Aric didn't like the idea of lying to the service, but the two would be on thin ice as it was. "You think they'll buy it?"

"Who knows, who cares? Right now I need a stiff drink and a few good reasons to remind myself why I don't hate you."

*"There was a craterous hole in the toilet wall,
big enough to fit a person through, and no sign of Yoshiko.
Painted on the wall in blood was
a message in Kaizen."*

Aric smiled. "First round is on me then?"

Percy slapped him on the shoulder again and they grabbed their coats. Percy hit the lights, and in the darkness, wondered which of the two men was worse. The one who let a trained killer get away because he couldn't see past her gender, or the one who was willing to put a bullet through a young woman's head because he could?

Tales of the Modern Realms
NEW · REGIME · PRESS · FICTION
NR
£0.46
Free!
A
STONE'S THROW
AWAY
A Grantia
Story
By Jack Harvey
JH2014

Modern Realms

A Stone's Throw Away

A Grantia Story

By Jack Harvey

Five Seven One was a lonely man. Once upon a time he had been the scourge of the realms. As one of the 3000 Mages, he had nearly brought all the realms to its knees, until his plans came to ruin when their enemies employed weapons of gunpowder and steam. The realms were a different place now, and it was all because of what they had failed to do.

Five Seven One had lived long past his human lifespan thanks to the powerful magics his compatriots had learned, but he remained hunted and feared even centuries later. He needed protection, and for that he needed allies. Five Seven One's talent was in the magic of creating life. He had birthed golems, constructs and homunculi for the war. Even now there were those of ill repute who would pay good money for emotionless creatures of clay and stone created for the express purpose of employing violence.

Over the years Five Seven One had worked for gangsters and despots, corrupt businessmen and amoral playboys, but always he had to remain in the shadows, hidden away underground or in desolate wastelands. Though many thought him long dead, there was still a bounty on his head that would satisfy any man ten times over.

Loneliness, it was his burden and his alone. It had been a long time since he had felt the touch of a lover. He feared he would be driven insane through solitude, until one day an idea struck him. Though Five Seven One had dared not conceive it in the past, he knew that there were ways, dark and old, that one could use to create life. He would mould a companion, the perfect woman, by giving a little bit of his own life in return.

Grantia was the result of this ritual. He had built her carefully out of fine grey granite. Slabs of the rock slid smoothly where one would expect to find muscle and bone. Her face a composition of expressive lines, her eyes cut from brightest emerald. Her head was bald, for now, he would procure a wig later, but otherwise she was a masterpiece of design.

However, like the 3000 Mages he fought alongside, his plans were all for naught. Grantia had everything he had wanted, conscious thought, a personality, human desires, but the ritual had worked all too well. When Five Seven One had brought her into being with his own life force, she had inherited his own longing for female companionship too. There was little in him she saw in her own desires.

A month later to the day Five Seven One finally caved in frustration, and tried to take what he felt was his by force. This ended with his skull cracked open over the tiled floor. Grantia threw his lifeless corpse over her shoulder, marched miles to claim the bounty, and started her life proper. A wig never did grace her grey stone head.

***

The atmosphere surrounding the summit of the Royaux Mountains was far from similar to the icy wasteland that Five Seven One had placed his hideaway, but the bitter cold was still enough to remind Grantia of those days long ago. She couldn't feel the cold of course, but she was still aware of it. The frosting she had to wipe away from her gemstone eyes being one such troubling reminder.

In the years that followed, Grantia had found work contracted to her by ORTO, the Old Realms Treaty Organisation, an intergovernmental military alliance of nations based out of the Old Realms, and some from the new. ORTO could not use her for espionage, as she was far too unique for that. Her trouble with discipline made her a poor fit for the military. After months of back and forth, ORTO finally gave her purpose; Monster hunting.

Grantia pulled her frosted up binoculars out of her sleeveless leather jacket and scanned the rocky peaks. She unclipped a length of rope from her belt, reinforced to support her weight, and measured the distance. She marched over to a four foot stone monolith. To the untrained eye it may well have been just a part of the geography, but Grantia could tell by it's shape it had once been worked by living hands. She tied the rope around the rock, grasped it tight and wrapped it over her shoulder. She pulled. It slid towards her with ease, clearly designed for creatures of flesh and blood.

The rock had given way to a descending tunnel. An old tomb from Arthur's reign, though long since looted. Grantia could see marks and indentations where gemstones and gold would once have graced the rock in celebration of it's occupant - no doubt lacing the coffers of some mercenary or greedy aristocrat now.

Whilst, legally speaking, ORTO was not allowed to order hits on living beings, sentient or otherwise, but as such creatures often graced the crypts and catacombs of various lands, they contracted Grantia out to archaeological organizations. Any creature deemed a threat to historical sites or artefacts were fair game.

If a dangerous creature refused to heed her warning, be it a Lich or Hydra, Chimera or Gorgon, Grantia was well within her remit to exterminate with extreme prejudice.

Dragons though, were out of bounds. No risk of that here though, at least as as far as she could see. Grantia illuminated the passage with her torch. Whoever had stripped the tomb of it's precious shiny bounty, they weren't adding it to a dragon's hoard.

Grantia had been sent to the settlements that circled the Royaux Mountains after the disappearance of several men. There were only one or two disappearances at first, but soon people were going missing almost nightly, and nobody was more concerned about this than the executives of Ayoade Global; a diamond corporation from The Golden Lands who had expanded their operation into The Old Realms.

Like most corporations they were bleeding the local workforce dry, but if anybody was going to be responsible for employee fatalities they would make damn sure it was in the name of profits.

Though it had seemed Grantia's investigation had again come upon a dead end. This had been the third tomb in the region she had checked, and like the others there was no sign of monstrous intent, just empty tombs, long looted.

As she stepped forwards, Grantia felt something depress beneath her foot. A click and a bang made her pull out her revolver instinctively, but she had misjudged the threat. A steel tipped spear shot out and stabbed into her arm. It broke off once it came into contact with her stone body, but a little bit of her own shoulder blade had been chipped away with it. She grimaced with the kind of pain only she could understand, but as she rubbed at the damage she knew it could be repaired easily. Still, she knew now it would be better to be careful, there may be other snares along the way that could do more permanent damage.

Grantia stopped. *Traps. Why had the tomb's previous visitors deemed it necessary to reset the traps?* All the other tombs had been disarmed, yet this one's defences had been reactivated. If Grantia had a heart it would have begun to beat with excitement, but without she still managed to enjoy some smug satisfaction.

She traversed the cave a little slower this time, taking care to avoid anything underfoot that looked a little conspicuous. Shortly, she came to a large rectangular room. The floor was covered in pressure plates, and it would be impossible to traverse without setting foot on some of them. She could see that the plates had runes calved into them, but their significance was not apparent. Once it seems the room would have been adorned with artwork featuring a riddle to accompany it, but unfortunately time and looters had rendered it indecipherable.

No point in attempting to solve the room's puzzle, no point in a running jump either, she was far too heavy. Grantia concluded that there must be a way to bypass the trap. Whoever had been here first had been able to reactivate it, so there had to be a mechanism somewhere on this side with which to tamper. She doubled back to retrieve the broken spear and leaned forward to poke one of the pressure plates.

Nothing happened at first. Then, shortly, Grantia heard a brief hiss. Suddenly the walls either side slammed together quickly. After a brief moment's pause there was another hiss and the walls slowly slid back into place. A clicking, clanking sound confirmed some kind of gear was rewinding the trap. Grantia couldn't rely on her fortitude to get her through this one.

The hiss though, that confirmed that the trap was driven by the displacement of air. There must have been a mechanism somewhere that builds up air pressure to push the walls together. *Yet how to get to it?*

Grantia's hand carefully followed the contours of the wall. Slowly, looking for cracks, gaps. It wasn't long until she found one, a tablet that would once have displayed a great tale, now worn and defaced beyond value. She didn't feel too bad then when she made a fist, pulled her arm back, and punched through the crumbling stone. On the other side was a small shaft, with only foot holds to help one climb down. Hardly a challenge for her though, she had just climbed a mountain range without breaking a figurative sweat.

Below, the mechanism was crammed into the rock and soil. A large balloon of some resilient hide, could even have been dragon, contained ancient air that it would blow into another above it. Bolted firmly to the walls, a brass mechanism of gears and cranks revealed the complex workmanship that kept the traps functional.

The hide was likely treated to withstand blades, claws and the ravages of time. Grantia pulled out her 44. and blew a large hole all the way through. It deflated sadly, pathetically.

Grantia made it across the room with only the left side wall impotently thrusting forward in a futile attempt to stop her. The tomb's further traps were easier to avoid, and sooner than she expected she had made it to the central room.

Grantia couldn't smell, and for once she was glad of this. By an old coffin she had found what remained of the missing men. The bodies looked as though they had decayed over centuries, but their workman’s overalls were still clean and new.

"A steel tipped spear shot out and stabbed into her arm. It broke off once it came into contact with her stone body, but a little bit of her own shoulder blade had been chipped away with it."

Amongst the bodies were masses of diamonds, so whatever was responsible liked to mix death with extravagance.

She put her hand to the floor, felt around. She could see it in the dust and gravel. She would have smelt it too if she could. A sickening yellow and red. Salty in texture. A ring of sulphur graced the floor. Within Grantia could make out various runes and scripts. She couldn't read it, but she recognised the language. Coupled with the sulphur it could mean only one thing; she was dealing with a demon.

***

The denizens of the Royaux Mountains were a humble people, but they loved sophistication. Mostly human, with a modest number of half-elves in their population, they had once been travellers, with no nation to call their own. Few knew what had finally persuaded them to settle down, in the cold north of all places, but settle they did, and they had thrived there ever since.

It was night by the time she had returned from her treacherous journey, and Grantia had returned to Romahold to report her progress to the archaeologists. She had met up with them in the northernmost part of the city, where the upper classes would hold great balls and parties on the weekend. Finding them wasn't difficult. The fashion in this part of the realms was greatly influenced by coloured silks and gold jewellery. Dr Steven Dunstead, by contrast, was a bland sight dressed in his simple tweed jacket.

As Grantia approached, she noticed that Dunstead wasn't alone, he had been joined by a group of similarly dressed individuals. Grantia groaned. Dunstead alone could talk and talk, she didn't like the idea of being saddled by even more academics.

“Ah, Grantia,” the bespectacled doctor greeted. “Come over. He's waiting for you.”

Grantia gave Dunstead a puzzled look. “He?”

“David Delcourt, vice president of Ayoade Global.” Dunstead started off into space and scratched at a bald patch on his head. “Or... something. He's come to check on your progress.”

Grantia sighed. Corporate. Suddenly the idea of being saddled with the history buffs didn't come across as bad as she thought.

“He's waiting for you in a private room, just by the entrance. You can...”

“It's okay Doctor,” Grantia said with a smile, and patted him on the shoulder. Her heavy stone hand knocked him a little off balance. “I can find my own way.”

Grantia made her way to a small room which seemed to be used as a lock up or some kind of cloak room. Whatever it was for, this David Delcourt had made it his own, ordering the place to look as though it were some kind of office. If Grantia didn't know better she would assume he was a regular patron.

He pretended not to notice her at first, a common tactic used by business men in an attempt to assert superiority. After a moment he smiled and stood.

Grantia held out her hand, and the man in the suit reciprocated. It seemed as though he was the kind of person that would have kissed a normal woman on both cheeks, but Grantia was not a normal woman. He shook her hands firmly, and did not wince at her stony grip. An impressive feat in and of itself.

He wore sharp black suit, a red ascot tied around his neck. He was handsome, classically so, and he radiated wealth, even more than the aristocrats that frequented this place. What stood out to Grantia though, was his skin. Ayoade Global was a company from The Golden Lands, one of the biggest in fact. Grantia was expecting a dark skinned gentleman from the continent. Tanned or not, there was no way this individual had been born south of Apolla.

Delcourt noticed that she was distracted. He smiled. “I know. You were probably expecting a Golden Lander right?”

Grantia nodded. “How does someone from The Old Realms end up supervisor for an entire operation?"

He laughed a little, though Grantia hadn't intended to amuse. "Would you believe me if I told you I was just that talented?"

A stone eyebrow slid up Grantia's forehead.

"No, I suppose not." Delcourt walked round a makeshift desk. "Truth be told I married into the business, and when Ayoade wanted to expand operations to The Old Realms they decided to send someone who would be more familiar."

It was a reasonable enough explanation she supposed. "Well, anyway I imagine you'd like to know how I'm getting along?" she said.

"Of course, of course." He said, leaning back onto the desk casually. "The families of the deceased are eager for some conclusive facts. It's the very least we can offer to help them get on with the rest of their lives.

He had a grin like a snake. Grantia could tell just by looking he didn't give a damn about the workers.

"Well, I've scoured the tombs. The last I got to had pretty substantial evidence that what we're dealing with is a demon."

"I see," Delcourt said, expressing little emotion or interest. "But you can handle that right?"

Grantia sighed and closed her eyes. "Mr Delcourt, what we're dealing with here isn't as simple as a Gorgon or a Basilisk. Demons are smart, deceptively intelligent creatures. I have the tools necessary to take care of things, but I'd seriously recommend seeking the services of a professional cleric. They are much more qualified to deal with something of this nature."

Delcourt winced. Grantia could tell he was already counting the cost in his head. "But you and ORTO, you already have an obligation to the historical society surely? Those tombs date back to Arthur's day."

Grantia shrugged. "Quite frankly there's very little of historical interest left in those old caves. If they held anything of worth it would have been looted long ago." She grinned. "Who knows, those cuff-links you're wearing probably have more material worth."

"What are you saying?" Delcourt stood, frustration in his voice. "That you're done here?"

Grantia bobbed her stone head. "That's up to Dunstead and his friends, but short of coming across an Aether ruin we'll probably be all be gone once the weekend is through."

Delcourt put a balled fist to his mouth, as if to hold back some ill advised comment. After a few moments his smile returned. He put his hand in his pocket, and pulled out a few bank notes.

"What's this?" Grantia said. It was pitifully small if he was attempting a bribe.

"You only have a few more nights here. I'd hate for you to depart without sampling the delights of Romahold's festivities." He tucked the banknotes into her jacket. "Have a few drinks on me. It's the least I can grant you for your services."

Grantia began to feel a little uncomfortable. "I'm only here to protect the Doctor's dig sites. Anything else that may come about would be nothing more than a happy accident."

Delcourt nodded. He held out his hand. They shook again, though it felt far from amicable. He leaned in close and softly spoke into her ear. "You should try the baby tomatoes they serve here. The things taste divine."

Now feeling wholly uncomfortable, Grantia made her way to the door.

****

"So. How did it go?" Asked Dunstead.

"Apart from the fact that he was doing the usual millionaire creep routine? About as well as could be expected." Grantia looked around, his associates had vanished. "He was hoping we'd be staying long enough to deal with the disappearances."

Dunstead sighed himself. It was the first time that Grantia had seen the eager historian look tired. He shook his head. "I understand your employers have a little unwritten agreement that we egg heads bring you along to take care of any... undesirable presence."

Grantia shrugged. She didn't hide what she was here to do.

"But the treaty still states that we can only stay to secure locations of significant historical importance. Save coming across an Aether ruin..."

"Yeah, I already gave him that line." Grantia said.

Dunstead shook his head again. "My hands are tied. I know you, Ayoade, and ORTO themselves will want this creature taken care of, but It's not in your official job description to hunt monsters. I can't justify the cost of holding my group here any longer on those grounds."

"Yeah, I understand," Grantia agreed, though she was frustrated. "Tell me, where have all the others gone?"

Dunstead's smile returned. "Taking in a little of the Romahold extravagance. Who am I, with my boring lectures on buttons, to stand in the way of the beautiful Lady DeGray?"

Grantia had noticed the woman he was talking about, another who stood apart from the locals. She was tall, slender, her legs seemed to go on forever and her curves were that of a courtesan but she had the face of noble birth. She wore jewellery that drew the eye to all the places a man was interested in. She wore a dress that revealed far more than was expected of a woman, yet had such confidence that nobody would dare accuse her of dressing inappropriately.

Beauty was in the eye of the beholder of course. Grantia was not the kind of person to be captivated by a bit of bare flesh, but the woman had piqued her curiosity. Dunstead had been right though, a historian, even a high flying expert, was nothing in the face of such a woman. "Who is that?" Grantia asked him.

"Lady Dantes DeGray. A well to do sort who moved here a few years ago. Word is she's been looking for a husband to share her not inconsiderable wealth with, but has remained unmarried all this time. The local fellas' treat her as though she's some kind of walking lottery, though whether its the money or her body they are after I'll leave for you to decide."

"Hmmm," Grantia stroked her stony chin. "I'll catch up with you in a bit Doctor."

"What? Where are you going?" Exclaimed the doctor, trying to bustle after her.

"Chasing a few leads," she said, and she barged her way into the crowd.

Lady DeGray was at the bar now surrounded by potential suitors vying for attention. Grantia shoved her way through, and suddenly an unstoppable force had met an immovable object. There had been sideways glances towards Grantia from the moment she had arrived, but now she was up close the men could not do nothing but stare.

She understood, she was one of a kind. Wherever she went people would be curious. Lady DeGray however, remained cool, even in the face of losing attention.

"And who might you be?" Lady DeGray purred.

Grantia pulled out her identification. "Agent Grantia, ORTO department of historical preservation."

"Deliciously fascinating," DeGray said with an air of polite disinterest. "I have seen many rock golems in my time but I had long thought they were nothing more than mindless brutes. You appear to be much more..." DeGray stopped for a moment and her eyes lingered over Grantia's body, "...articulated."

"It's a long story." Grantia said, shoving her identification back into her jacket. "You seem to have a fairly unique view on the goings on around here. I was just wondering if I could ask you a few questions?"

"Hmmm," Lady DeGray mused as she stroked the long hair of one of the men surrounding her. Grantia watched curiously as her sharp fingernails combed through his locks. "I don't know. I do have prior commitments tonight.."

"Tell you what," Grantia put her hand on DeGray's shoulder, a little too forcefully than she intended. “You tell me your story, and I'll tell you mine.”

Lady DeGray wasn't threatened, instead smiled as though Grantia were another suitor. “Very well.” She leaned forwards, he voice a little lower. “I have my own table and booth if it's privacy you require.”

Grantia smiled back, politely, and nodded.

“Very well. Manuel!” she shouted over to one of the staff. “Have my table ready and three rounds of Tanandos.”

The men sighed, begging her to stay, but she waved them off.

“Now, now, gentlemen, you have my attention most every night. Allow me this slight dalliance for once.” She took Grantia by the arm, coiling around her. She led her through to a quieter part of the bar, lit only by deep red lamps and candles.

They were seated, and brought drinks and olives with baby tomatoes. Lady DeGray began to eat.

“I'm sorry Lady DeGray...”

“Call me Dantes my dear,” she said, cutting Grantia off.

“Dantes. I appreciate your hospitality but I'm afraid I don't drink.”

“Can't, or won't?”

Grantia didn't need to eat, drink or sleep, but she had been created to be a companion, and that meant she had to be capable of experiencing earthly pleasures. She had only tried to drink a few times, and even then it was not in great quantities. Maybe she had been designed to allow for the consumption of libations, she had never put that to the test before. She picked up the drink and sipped at it out of courtesy. The sensation was dulled on her stone tongue, but still noticeable.

“So, what is it you wish to talk about?” Lady DeGray asked, chewing on an olive.

Grantia didn't stand on ceremony. “Let's start from the beginning shall we? I was told you moved here a few years ago. A strange thing for a lady to do, moving to the outskirts of the realms where nobody had ever heard of her.”

Grantia spoke with an inquisitorial tone but if Lady DeGray felt she were under inquiry she didn't show any nerves, simply smiling and looking down at her drink. "My family hails from Avalon. You probably know they think little of nobles there, after they executed most of the monarchy during the industrial revolution."

"But that was generations ago, it's a little late to be going into exile now isn't it?"

"Oh that's not what it is," Dantes brushed her hair back, reclining in her seat. "I simply grew tired of Avalon, boring and grey. I had the money and wanted more interesting scenery. So I left with my family entitlement for pastures new."

"Why here?"

"Why not?"

"It's cold and desolate," said Grantia, thinking back to the days of her creation. "So much more than Avalon, and it's not very well travelled, there are few that come here from the wider realms."

"But the people are so interesting," Dantes said, her face lighting up. "So unspoiled by others. It is places like this that you find things that are... truly unique." She smiled softly, gazing once more upon Grantia's stone complexion.

"Hmnf," Grantia grumbled, she could tell Lady DeGray was holding back. "And what about the recent disappearances, do they not worry you?"

"A sad state of affairs," she said evasively. "I knew many of those men, a few of them had proposed to me several times. But one cannot live one's life in a bubble. To live without risk is not to live at all."

"Any you haven't heard anything? No suspicions as to what might be responsible?"

"I am simply a lady with too much time and money on her hands, I have no experience in the more brutal side of man."

She was lying. Grantia could tell, but for some reason she remained uncritical. There was something in Dantes that she liked, an optimism, a hypnotic quality. When she spoke, it was as if her words were taking on a life of their own. Maybe Grantia was susceptible to alcohol after all, because without realising it she had begun to stroke Dante's leg with her foot. She quickly drew it back, embarrassed.

"My, so you *swing that way* do you?" Dantes smiled.

"I.. ugh," Grantia flustered. *What had come over her?* "I'm sorry, it was an accident."

"No need to apologize," Dantes leaned forward. "A lady knows how to be discreet."

Grantia coughed.

"Anyway. I've reiterated my tale, bore that it is. Now it's your turn."

Over the course of a few more drinks Grantia related her tale and, to her pleasure, Dantes seemed genuinely interested. They talked through the night, and though Grantia tried a few more times to catch Dantes out, she gave away nothing more about the missing men. Grantia didn't mind though, for the first time in far too long she was enjoying herself, aided by her discovery of alcohol, and Dantes was, if nothing else, as fun to talk to as she was to look at.

As night crept on it was time to retire. As Dantes bid farewell, it seemed for a moment that she was going to make a pass at Grantia, but the flirtatious dialogue was maybe all in her mind. Dantes gave her a non-committal kiss on the cheek and waved her goodnight.

It didn't matter though, the alcohol was quickly being purged from Grantia's system and her thoughts were clear again. Dantes may have thought that she could convince with an Avalonian accent, but in truth Grantia could tell it was more like a Wessex one. An easy mistake to make, for somebody who didn't know the distinction.

She retrieved her weapons from the concierge at the door, then carefully began tailing Dantes back to her home. Though she didn't have any evidence yet, she would bet her life that Dantes was the one she was looking for.

"There was something in Dantes that she liked, an optimism, a hypnotic quality. When she spoke, it was as if her words were taking on a life of their own."

****

What were demons? Were they dark parallels of gods and angels, created at the dawn of time to balance absolute good with absolute evil? Were they physical manifestations of the realm's worst excesses? Rage, greed, lust, wrath? Or were they simply creatures of habit, born of a different plane of existence, that followed its own rules, customs and prejudices?

Grantia didn't know, nor did she really need to. All she needed to know was how to banish one back to the hells. Before attending the party she had loaded her gun with sanctified bullets, blessed by seven different churches and cast in silver. If Dantes was a demon she was surely a lesser kind. A succubus most likely. She would be no match for Grantia's ordinance.

Dantes lived in an exquisite apartment. It was a mix of modern minimalism and traditional carved wood. Grantia slowly ascended the stone steps that ran up to the door, having to take extra care due to her weight. Finally at the front, she pulled out her pistol and tried to peer through the frosted glass. Nothing. She moved to try the handle.

Suddenly it opened and there was Dantes, strikingly dressed as ever. She was not surprised, it was almost as if she expected Grantia to be there. Grantia hid her gun behind her back quickly.

"My my, couldn't stay away could you?" she said seductively.

"I.. was just making sure you made it home safe. Can't be too careful what with the disappearances of late," she stammered, caught off guard.

Dantes ignored Grantia's protests. "Come in," she said. She was just as hospitable as earlier.

She led Grantia through to a dimly lit living room. An open fire roared beside the modern furniture. She could see that the lights were electric, not gas, which was still the common light source for most of the realms.

"You've probably figured it out by now," Dantes said, "I'm not what I say I am."

Grantia thumbed back the hammer on her .44, her hands still clasped behind her back.

Dantes held out her arms and snapped her fingers. The lights flickered. With little ceremony her skin turned a deep red, and her hair receded so that it ran along only the centre of her head, flanked by two long sharp horns. More obvious though was the long pointed tail that extended from her spine, and the bile coloured wings that sprouted from her back.

“Sit,” she said calmly, and patted a cushion next to her.

Grantia didn't know why she didn't just shoot Dantes there and then. Instead, she shoved the gun into it's holster and sat down.

“I suppose you're here to kill me?” Dantes said, surprisingly calm.

“That was the idea.”

“You don't have to, you know. My intent here is not malicious.”

Grantia laughed without humour.

“It's true. I am not here by choice. I was banished, chose the wrong side in a war few will ever know about. If I were to return to the hells there would be worse waiting for me. So instead I decided to have fun for as long as I could.” Dantes' long fingernails began stroking down the leather of Grantia's jacket.

Grantia showed little sympathy. She stood, abruptly. “Fun? Every man you take to bed dies.”

“Yes,” nodded Dantes with a little self awareness. “Yes they do. Do you know how that makes me feel?”

All joy and humour had dropped from the succubus's face now. Grantia knew better than to fall for the manipulations of a creature from hell, but she felt a little pity. She knew from personal experience what Dantes was feeling.

“You're lonely,” Grantia said. Her disposition hardened. “Boo fucking hoo. Aren't we all?”

Dantes looked at the floor and laughed humourlessly. “How long has it been for you?”

"How long since what?"

"Since you last had... companionship?" Dantes' eyes lingered on Grantia, following the line of her unconventional frame.

It had been a while, Grantia had had lovers in the past, but given her constitution very few would stay around for the physical commitments. "Long enough," she said.

"Well then." Dantes got to her feet and walked over to Grantia. She put her arms round Grantia's shoulders, moving slowly under the fur lined jacket. "No man could survive a night with me, but I reckon *you* just might be in with a chance."

Grantia shook her head, but she didn't force Dantes away. "You think I'm going to fall for that one?"

"It's true. Golems by their very design are immune to all magics, and I'm willing to bet that pistol of yours is loaded with sanctified bullets. You don't tire and you don't need to sleep. You're more than a match for this weak little creature from a bygone era."

Grantia put her hands around Dantes' head and forced their lips together. It was an odd experience for the both of them, stone on demon's flesh, but it worked. Something Dantes had said earlier had stuck with Grantia. Might as well have fun for as long as they could.

****

Dantes woke to see Grantia getting dressed. It was the first time she had awoken from a night of lovemaking without having a corpse to deal with. Savouring the moment, she leaned over and put her arms around Grantia, and stroked the chip in her shoulder.

Grantia stood, without reciprocating this time, and pointed her pistol at Dantes' head.

Dantes lay back in bed, not taking Grantia seriously. "So you're going to kill me now? Was I really that out of practice?" Dantes joked, displaying mock disappointment.

" It was an odd experience
for the both of them, stone on
demon's flesh, but it worked. Something Dantes had
said earlier had stuck with Grantia. Might as well
have fun for as long as they could."

"The sob story worked for a while, but I'm not going to fall for it. Your magics will only get you so far."

"What are you talking about darling?" Dantes now sounded a little more worried, as Grantia pulled the hammer back on her pistol. Dantes grabbed the sheets and covered her body.

"Even if all of what you said was sincere, maybe you are as lonely as I am, but that doesn't excuse the deaths of seventeen men."

"The missing men?" Dantes said in fear. "You think that was me?"

Grantia laughed. "Oh please. You're going to tell me that it wasn't?"

"Grantia, darling, I haven't bedded a man since my banishment. You think I'd jeopardise what I have here like that? Why do you think I revealed myself to you?"

"What? Am I supposed to believe it's someone else then? *Another* demon? What would they have to gain by coming here, doing this? Who else would have the allure to draw those men to their deaths?"

For once, Dantes was lost for words. "I don't know."

Grantia pointed the gun and closed one eye to get a better aim. Square between the eyes. Simple. "For the record it was the accent. Demons can't mimic mortals they haven't experienced first hand, and we're a long way from Avalon."

Dantes lowered her head, resigned to her fate, black tears beginning to trickle down her cheeks. Grantia's stone fingers slowly began to depress the trigger.

"Oh shit." Grantia stopped. "It isn't you."

Dantes looked up, she didn't say anything.

"But I think I know who it is." Grantia threw some clothes over at Dantes. "Come on."

***

Grantia kicked the door down. Easy enough when you're made out of granite. David Delcourt and the two ladies he was in bed with looked over in surprise.

"Ladies, go." Grantia pointed a huge trench gun at him. "You, stay."

The ladies departed, and a now modestly dressed Dantes, back in human form, came to Grantia's side.

Delcourt sat at the end of the bed, smile on his face and began clapping slowly. "Oh bravo, bravo. Which one of you figured me out? I doubt it was you Dantes, you were always such a fool. It must have been you dear Grantia. How did you do it?"

"It wasn't difficult. A man from the Old Realms married his way into Ayoade's corporate board. Not impossible, just improbable."

"May I add that it wasn't so much of an oversight," he said charismatically. "I felt that the workers would be quicker to trust one of their own. Trust is such an important thing in this line of business."

"Enough bullshit, Martellus," Dantes said with venom, revealing her adversaries true name. "Show yourself."

Delcourt smiled and twirled his hand, there was a blast of smoke, and in his place was a creature twice his size, skin as red as Dantes herself. Martellus was a large muscular creature, bull horns spiralled around his massive under bite. Spines and thorns grew out of his flesh.

"I presume you came prepared?" Martellus tapped the barrel of Grantia's trench gun with a spiked talon.

"The shells are packed with the ashes of saints from seven different denominations."

"That'll do it," he said without fear.

"Ayoade Global never even knew about this did they?" She asked.

"Of course not," he laughed. "This was all my doing. I sensed a weakness in the space between worlds where once I had banished Dantes. I stripped the tombs of gold and sold it on the black market. Reinvented myself as a businessman. I told the locals I was working for Ayoade because they were more than happy to accept good fortune as truth."

*" Martellus was a large,
muscular creature, bull horns spiraled
around his massive under bite. Spines and thorns
grew out of his flesh."*

“And you led the workers away and force fed them diamonds till they choked.”

“Such a wonderful jest,” Martellus said with a grin sleazier even than that of his human form.

“Why?” said Grantia in disbelief. “What was all this in aid of?”

“To torment Dantes of course! I had grown so bored in the hells. I couldn't confront her directly, even in her weakened state. I set all of this up so that she would take the fall for my crimes, and be returned to the hells ready and waiting.”

“As vile as the day you were spawned Martellus,” Dantes said.

He laughed, and turned back to Grantia. “So. I suppose you'll want to hear why...”

Grantia pulled the trigger and Martellus' entire upper body exploded across the room. Dantes instinctively covered her eyes. When she opened them again she could see Matellus' remains were already turning to ash.

“I've heard quite enough for today,” Grantia said, and she propping the trench gun over her shoulder she turned to Dantes. “Come on. If we work fast we can reverse the summoning circle and he'll have no way of coming back.”

Before she could storm out the room, Dantes grabbed her by the arm.

“Wait a moment,” she said. “He'll be back. You can't keep a creature as vile as Martellus in the ninth circle forever. He'll scuttle out of his hole eventually and he won't be sunshine and rainbows.”

“What is it you're trying to say?”

“I won't be able to stay here.” The succubus looked down, a little nervous. “Could I...”

Grantia put her arm around Dantes. “Yes,” she said simply.

Dantes lay her head across Grantia's shoulder gently as they walked into the sunlight. Grantia didn't know what the future held, but at the very least the two of them might be able to stave off loneliness for just one more day.

Tales of the Modern Realms
NEW · REGIME · PRESS · FICTION ·
NR
DEATH AND POLITICS
£0.46
Free!
A
Leo Wounded Bear
Story
By Jack Harvey
JH
2014

Modern Realms

Death and Politics

A Leo Wounded Bear Story

By Jack Harvey

Leo Wounded Bear finished cleaning his side-arm. He had daydreamed through it. Second nature to him. He was a soldier once, but nowadays made a living as a bodyguard for Councilman Onatha. Still, he dressed prepared for combat, ever ready for action. Most who knew him said he worried far more than he should

"Your nerves betray you young one. Pray tell what is on your mind?" The creature said, hiding in shadow.

"You already know what is on my mind," Leo replied. The creature had arrived unannounced, but he had become so accustomed to it's visits that he was rarely startled.

The creature was known by many names. Changeling, Mimic, Shapeshifter. To Leo's people, it was Hoklonote, a creature that had one foot in this world and one in the next. A trickster that could read peoples thoughts. It's intentions were always unclear, but it long had an interest in Leo, an interest he knew he could exploit. The creature had chosen to appear as a hairy elongated humanoid, with the decomposing head of a dog. Hollow sockets stared at him out from the darkness.

"You fly far tomorrow young one, far from your native lands. You fear the Old Realmers?"

"I do not fear the Old Realmers. I do not hate them either, it is just that their ignorance irritates me."

One of the things that Leo had found from his work in the world of diplomacy was how easy it was for foreign nations to misunderstand his people and their ways.

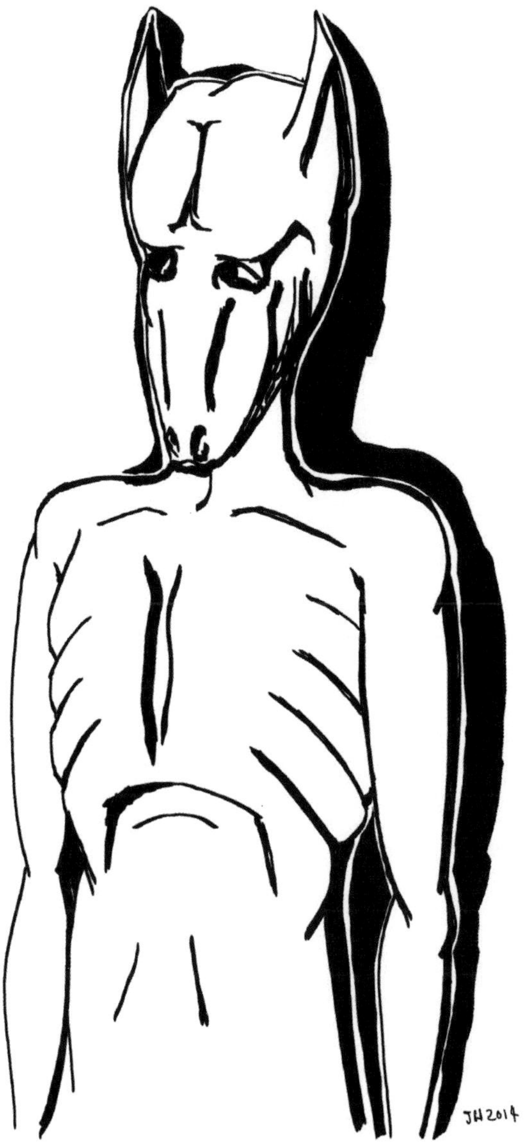

"The creature had chosen to appear
as a hairy elongated humanoid, with the
decomposing head of a dog. Hollow sockets
stared at him out from the darkness."

“They even insist on referring to The Circle as *The Circle of Druids*,” Leo laughed, “Druid is an Avalonian word. It is their own creation. The Circle is composed of shaman, medicine men and conjurers. Yet they still insist on playing by their own rules, not ours.”

“Are they truly your people? You are not a native of the Wendiga?” the creature asked. A touchy subject, since Leo was a son of the plains, not the forests.

“No,” he said confidently, “But the distinction only makes the ignorance more insufferable. Why are you here old one?”

A sickly breath left the the Hoklonote's withered lips before it spoke. “You travel tomorrow to Malana, Bascilicata for trade negotiations. You will be enjoying the hospitality of Fernando Carlita.”

“Enjoying?” Leo spat. “He is a rich fat animal. He only hosts these meetings to treat foreign dignitaries like personal exhibits. We are nothing but curiosities to him.”

“But go you will, because Onatha is the chief of agriculture, and the people need their food.”

Leo nodded, there had been a population boom over the last couple of generations, and the Wendiga were not a warlike people. They would happily pay when others would fight, but it takes a clever person to make sure you are not paying too much.

“A man will be there. I know not who, nor who he represents, but he will be there. He is armed with a weapon. An enchantment carved into the grip of his pistol. He is there to end Onatha's life.”

An image jumped into Leo's mind. A small sharp circle with three points extended. It was like a half star.

“Why?” Leo said, grimly. He was grateful for the warning, but he knew never to take a Hoklonote's advice at face value.

“Unknown, but not difficult to speculate. There is a tension between the council and The Circle. They resent the fact that outsiders treat The Circle as the de facto authority of the Spirit Lands. There are many who feel The Circle is becoming too influential."

"But the Councilman has The Circle's ear," Leo said, "As long at Onatha holds his position, tensions are eased."

"There are many who see a conflict amongst the Wendiga as profitable."

Leo was about to ask the Hoklonote what it meant by that, but without warning or ceremony it flitted out of existence. He had known the creature too long to bother crying for it to return. Instead he pondered upon it's warnings, and contemplated what it sought to gain.

It was to be a long weekend. Not in the good sense.

****

It had been a warm summer for the people of Wendiga. Not too hot, just about right. Blue skies, but with a gentle breeze. As Leo ascended the birch-wood spiral stairs he saw the great trees above him sway from side to side.

He could see most of the city from up here. The wooden buildings wound their way around the giant trees. Little clouds of smoke puffed out of one or two. It always worried Leo. From birth all Wendigans were taught to treat fire with respect. One loose flame could bring the whole city down, yet in all of it's five hundred year history it had yet to face such a tragedy.

Leo had reached the top of the steps now. Every time he ascended he would worry this would be the time it would leave him out of breath. His health was another thing he would often fret about. Yet each time he was shown to be as healthy as ever.

Leo tended to worry about a lot of things.

He opened the door to the building. It was a quiet, simple room. Odd that this was where all information ultimately went through. Though the printers were on the other side of the city, the information to be printed was all decided here.

Political and social careers lived and died by what went on in these rooms.

Odd that there didn't seem to be anybody around. Leo rang a chime hanging from the window by the desk.

A young woman emerged from a back room. She smiled when she saw him.

"Leo. It's great to see you again."

"Hi Mari," he said, smiling for the first time in what had felt like years. "Where is everyone?"

"News just broke about Galawain stepping down from The Circle. Everyone and their moose wants to be the one to get the exclusive. You know how unpopular he was."

"And he was an outsider."

"The one thing nobody wants to point out." She held out her hands. "So they had to leave the little apprentice girl behind to keep an eye on things."

Leo sighed.

"Well if it makes any difference they won't have me around for much longer," she said. "I'm quitting in two months. Going to Gia's Landing to study."

Leo was taken aback, Mari was one of the few familiar faces he knew these days. "You're leaving for New Dawn?"

"Not for too long, but I'm sick of being overlooked here. Maybe I'll pick up some stories and they'll finally start listening."

Leo nodded. "Well I hope it all works out for you."

"Thanks Leo." Her smile beamed again. "So... what was it you came here for?"

"Well I was hoping to speak to somebody who knew a thing or two about enchantments, but I can see my journey was wasted."

"As in weapon enchantments?" she said curiously.

"Yeah."

"I'm no expert or anything but I might be able to help you on that. Did a feature on the DPS last month, interviewed a few of their volunteers, a weapons expert."

Leo wondered if he was lucky or the Hoklonote knew he'd be coming here. He pulled out a scrap of paper that he had drawn the symbol onto. "Do you happen to know anything about this?"

Mari scanned the paper. "Yeah that's an enchantment alright. What colour is it supposed to be? Do you know?"

Leo strained to recall. "White I think."

Mari nodded. "It looks like an air enchantment. The guy told me that they're not really used anymore. In the old days they'd make weapons lighter but didn't really serve much purpose on modern firearms."

Leo was impressed, Mari always was good at recalling what she had learned. He decided to inquire further. "How would one go about such a thing?"

"Well, air magic supposedly originated in the east, so you'd probably have to lean the magic from a Magi."

"From the far side of the Golden Realms?" Leo asked?

"Yeah, but that being said, the guy told me that some elementally born people have a talent for it. We know that those born of elemental blood usually have an affinity for the magic of their element type. So I suppose it's possible an air born person could figure it out for themselves."

Leo nodded. It wasn't much but it was enough to give him a head start. "Thanks Mari."

Her friendly smile had turned into a sly grin. "You've had a tip off right? Somebody's gunning for Onatha. That's what this is about?"

She always was astute too. "That's confidential," Leo said sternly, before adding, "It's a crime they never promoted you."

She nodded, still grinning, but not saying anything further.

Leo opened the door out. "Good luck on your travels Mari."

****

Councilman Onatha always travelled without aides, and only Leo for protection. Many, Leo included, called this foolish, but Onatha always insisted that it was the best way.

"When a person walks into a room with fifteen bodyguards and twenty advisers it screams of arrogance. Before they even speak the others will already have made up their mind," Onatha said during their flight over. "The quiet two in the corner? Those two are humble. They could make the most outrageous demand in all the realms and it would still come out sounding reasonable."

Leo couldn't tell the councilman about the assassin. It would not be taken gracefully if people knew he associated with a Hoklonote. He had tried to get Onatha to take more men, but the councilman was having none of it. Onatha's priority was nailing the trade agreement, and he felt further protection would jeopardise that.

"You think the other delegates will be agreeable?" Leo asked.

"Most certainly. They know we do not need food, we have the power of earth magic granted by The Circle for that, but we do need resources." Onatha played with his hands excitedly. He always did that when he talked. "Fuel for the harvesters, fertilizer for the crops. It won't be hard, the Old Realmers heavily industrialized themselves decades ago. Most of them have forgotten what it was like to grow their own food."

"An exaggeration," Leo scoffed.

"That it is Leo, but one I do not state lightly. We have food in abundance, and as long as the Circle stays loyal to the continent then they cannot learn our secrets easily."

"Some would call that cruel." Leo said, grimly.

"Give a man a fish and he will eat for a day. Teach a man to fish and he has no further use for you," Onatha laughed. "This is no a fairy tale world Leo."

Leo knew that all too well. "I'm just keeping your mind sharp," he said.

There was a bullet with Onatha's name on it somewhere, waiting in an enchanted pistol. He wondered what the significance was. Enchantments were rarely seen in the modern realms, long gone out of use since flaming swords and lightning staffs were no longer needed. Leo continued, “This man, Carlita. I have heard many talk of him. They say he treats these gatherings like a freak show.”

“Worry not about this Carlita my friend. He is only the host, a playboy who thinks he can buy influence. In his Bascilicata that may be possible, but not to me. I only care about the talks, once they are finished we will depart.” Onatha turned carefully and pointed at Leo closely. “You just need to make sure you do your job. Keep me safe, and I will do my duty to the people.”

Leo nodded, but as always, he feared he was not up to the task.

****

“Take a shot from the bow. Go on, I have always been curious.”

Leo shook his head. “Mr Carlita, I have never trained in the use of a bow.”

“What! Never? I thought you Spirit Landers were brought up hunting bison upon the plains?”

Typical ignorant Old Realmer. “The Wendgia are forest dwellers Mr Carlita.”

“Bah, more boring than expected. Very well, I will have to go watch the Janissaries fly their carpets one more time.” Fernando Carlita waved Leo away. He was not as fat as Leo had been led to believe, and much more handsome. He radiated wealth, but this didn't make him any more likeable. Money was the man's only desirable quality.

Indeed the halls of his penthouse could attest to that. The entrance hallway was graced with a fountain flanked by two carved dragon skulls. These creatures were endangered now, but that didn't seem to stop Fernando displaying their remains with pride. The view of Malana from the roof was breathtaking, and it's tall skyscrapers even put Wendiga's own sprawling complexes to shame.

Leo walked past the pool, where Fernando's trophy wife kept herself amused. The bikini clad Aethena Carlita swam with an assortment of lady friends. Leo did not let his eyes linger like some did. To Wendigan men that kind of behaviour around women was deemed unseemly.

Instead he glanced up at the dignitaries on the next level. They were all talking Avalonian, as it was one of the most widespread languages thanks to King Arthur's crusades during the golden age.

Onatha seemed safe for now. There were only other dignitaries around the table. It was unlikely that an assassin would strike during the talks. Instead he motioned to the barman for a drink, and leaned over the glass barrier to enjoy the view.

The Vangarian Janissaries glided past on their flying carpets. Leo was modestly impressed. He had never seen the carpets of the desert legends before. It reminded him that The Circle could produce spectacles just as breathtaking.

"Bunch of amateurs," came an accented voice beside him. It was one of the other delegate's bodyguards. One from the flying city of Al' Fahja. If Leo recalled correctly he had introduced himself earlier as Nazim. Though he wore a red and white headscarf, Leo could see that beyond his tanned skin there was a trace of elven blood in him, probably second or third generation.

"You are not entertained?" Leo asked.

"Bah. The Vangarians have only known the art half as long as the people of Al' Fahja." Nazim said, his disgust exaggerated. "If Carlita thinks that this is skill then he should see what our carpet runners can do."

"Why didn't you..." Leo started, but was quickly cut off.

"Because my people aren't stupid enough to go around displaying their military capability for all to see. There are eyes watching you know?"

"Or listening," Leo said, partly as a joke, but partly for vigilance. He leaned back and looked over at the bar. There was a man seated there. He was middle aged, bearded and white. He wore a heavy brown jacket with fur lining, odd for the time of year. “Have you any idea who that man might be?”

“Him? Been here since we arrived. I think someone said he was with the Avalonian delegation. He has got his priorities right I can tell you that much.”

Leo looked back up at the delegates. The Avalonian government's foreign secretary was kicking up a fuss about something. He was an air born human with faintly translucent skin. A co-incidence? Leo had to wonder.

“So you are the Wendigan's bodyguard yeah?” Nazim continued, “You seem pretty miserable my friend. Are you not enjoying Signor Carlita's hospitality?”

“I find it hard to do this job without confronting the misery.” Leo replied wearily.

Nazim laughed. “Relax. Have another drink. Go talk to the fair Aethena if that's your poison. From what I've heard she’s no stranger to extra marital activities. Strapping young man like you shouldn't have any trouble.” He slapped Leo playfully on the chest. “That being said it looks like the barrel chested Avalonian's got there ahead of you.”

Leo turned to see Aethena talking flirtatiously with a tough looking bodyguard. Despite her enthusiasm, he still wore an uncomfortable grimace. Leo had little interest and turned away.

Nazim seemed to take personal insult to this. “Oh by the gods why do you Spirit Landers have to be so fucking stoic all the time?”

“I am not being stoic you desert dwelling hoople head.” Leo shot back. “I am being professional. You want raucous small talk then drop me a line when I'm off duty. For now I don't have time for anything but the job.”

“And a small whiskey it seems,” Nazim eyed Leo's now empty glass. Before the jab could find it's mark, shots were fired, and the two men turned in a panic. Nazim held his cool much better than Leo did.

"I am not being stoic you desert dwelling hoople head." Leo shot back. "I am being professional. You want raucous small talk then drop me a line when I'm off duty. For now I don't have time for anything but the job."

There were playful screams and giggles from the women as the Avalonian fired off a few more shots towards the bottles on the wall. His aim was awful, until a fifth shot finally found it's mark. Leo squinted to see if he could make out any markings on the grip, but the man was too far away.

“See what I mean? Surrounded by amateurs.” Nazim joked to ease the tension “I could have hit that bottle in one.”

“You like to boast a lot don't you?” Leo said. “You are a proud man.”

Nazim didn't seem to take offence. “One of my many sins. Alas, you know what the cult of Dread Lord Skafell preach?”

“You've got to sin to get saved,” the two recalled the common saying in unison.

Leo smiled. He hadn't realised he'd been doing it. To Nazim's credit the man didn't gloat. He slapped Leo on the chest again. “Let's go get a drink.”

The two left the railings to head back to the bar. Leo picked up the conversation quickly. “I thought the people of Al' Fahja did not touch alcohol. Something about it being against your religion.”

“Bah! You are thinking of the followers of Urak. A popular religion from my home, but not the only one. I am a follower of Passia, which means I get to eat drink and make love to whomever I want.”

“No doubt related to your elven heritage,” Leo nodded.

Nazim looked surprised. “Well spotted my friend. Though I confess I think I please the goddess far more than the stuffy elven kingdoms ever did.”

They had closed in on the bar now. The delegates were descending the nearby stairs, and they too were looking for libations. Noticing this, Nazim hopped forward, accidentally colliding with the Avalonian man from earlier.

“You'd be able to see where you were going if you didn't have that fucking towel on your head,” the man shot an uncomfortable slur, but Nazim took it in his stride.

“I don't know what you use for towels back in Avalon my friend,” he pointed to his head scarf. "Is this the kind of thing you use when your woman refuses to wash the dishes?"

The man didn't say anything, too surprised to think of a clever retort. He shuffled closer to the man in the brown jacket and Leo thought he caught them trading words. Nazim taxed his attention though, as the dark skinned half-elf had somehow managed to get them two whiskeys in the time it took Leo to blink.

"That was not very nice of him." Leo said.

"Old Realmers will always be that way. Don't let it get to you." Nazim laughed. He leaned over so that the Avalonian could hear him. "I'm still a better shot than him anyhow."

Leo spied Onatha approaching, he was chatting cordially to the Avalonian minister.

"So you imagine yourself a good shot?" he asked Nazim.

"Best in the city if I do say so myself," He answered not too seriously.

"You have your side-arm with you now?"

"Of course," Nazim said, smiling. "I would be a pretty lousy bodyguard without one."

Leo paused for a moment.

"Let me see it." He said, holding out his hand.

"What?" Nazim replied, a little confused.

"I want to see your pistol." Leo said again, his tone was more aggressive this time. Commanding.

Nazim's smile started to fade. "Why?" he asked.

Leo didn't grace him with an answer. The Spirit Lander's face was like stone, unmoving. A few people in the bar had noticed the tension, and the chattering began to die down.

"Show me your pistol," Leo commanded again.

Nazim looked around. Without knowing what Leo's game was he put his glass on a nearby ledge and slowly began to move his hand up to his jacket.

"A woman screamed.
Onatha gasped as he looked down the barrel of a gun.
Faster than a blink Leo whipped out
his pistol and fired."

Leo gritted his teeth and made his hand ready to go for his own. Slowly, slowly, Nazim reached under his armpit and began to withdraw. Leo's hand hovered over his holster. Nazim's hand came back into focus, concealing the grip of the pistol. Carefully now, he pulled it out of his jacket.

A woman screamed. Onatha gasped as he looked down the barrel of a gun. Faster than a blink Leo whipped out his pistol and fired.

****

The weapon clattered to the floor, a glowing white star shape etched into it's grip. The Avalonian bodyguard looked down at his broad chest and coughed up a gob of blood. Seconds later, he dropped to his knees and fell flat on his face.

Onatha sighed in relief. Nazim, not quite sure what had just happened, was frozen in place. His knuckles white as he held his own gun tight. Calming down, he returned his pistol to it's place of concealment.

"How did you know?" Asked Onatha, jogging towards Leo, none the worse for wear. "How did you know?"

"To be honest It could just have easily been Nazim." Leo looked at the half elf. "I thought it odd you singled me out for a drink. I guess you are just a polite guy after all."

This snapped Nazim out of his tension, and he smiled goofily.

"As for the Avalonian, I thought it was a little unusual for a bodyguard to be such a bad shot," Leo noted. "Which meant he was wielding a weapon he wasn't used to. An air enchantment means lighter bullets, and lighter bullets are harder to aim."

"If that was the case, then why bother with the air enchantment?" Nazim asked, finally coming up to speed.

"I suspect to incriminate you sir." Leo pointed to the foreign secretary he had seen earlier.

"Me?" the man said in shock.

"Elemental born people have a natural affinity for certain aspects of magic. I suspect the man intended to carry out his assassination covertly, and later plant the evidence. Hoped we would put two and two together and make five. Fortunately I managed to force his hand."

"A risky strategy Leo," said Onatha, "but a prudent one."

"Did you know the man?" Leo asked the foreign secretary.

"No. He was a last minute addition, one of my regular boys was otherwise indisposed."

"By the way things are going I imagine he's permanently indisposed," Nazim joked blackly, but nobody laughed.

Leo turned to the bar, and looked at the now empty seat the mysterious man in the jacket once graced. Long gone no doubt. If this man was as smart as Leo guessed, then the mystery would never be solved. Not for a long time at any rate.

The assassin's body began to leak blood over Carlita's miraculous marble floor. This debacle had irritated the millionaire, but was ultimately little more than an inconvenience to him. The Hoklonote's grim premonition had played out to it's grizzly end.

"My goodness. Oh dear lord. We're going to have to do an investigation." said the minister. "Why would anyone do such a thing?"

"Who can say?" Leo said, turning away from the gore. "Politics probably."

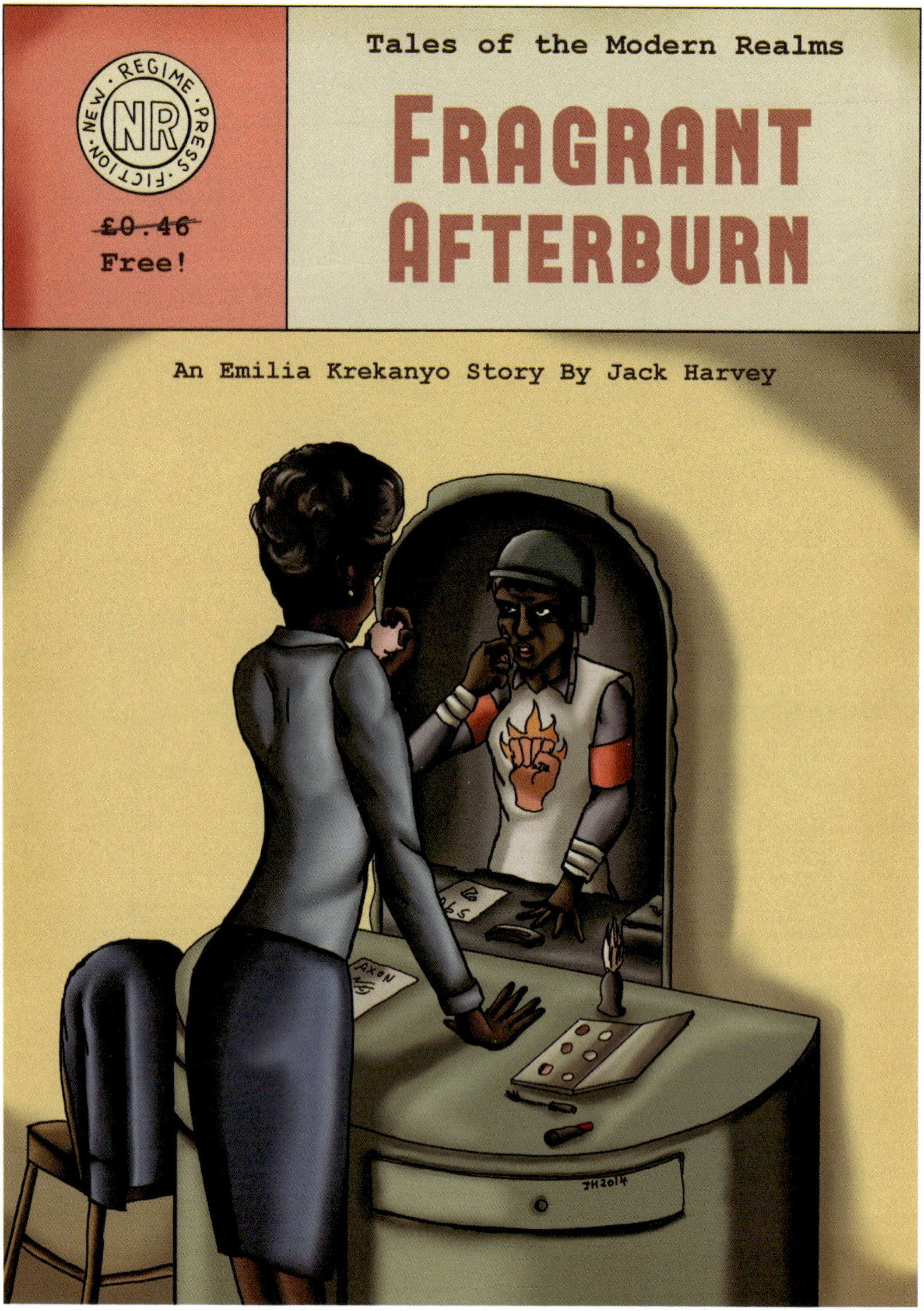
NEW · REGIME · PRESS · FICTION
NR
£0.46
Free!
Tales of the Modern Realms
FRAGRANT AFTERBURN
An Emilia Krekanyo Story By Jack Harvey
JH2014

Modern Realms
Fragrant Afterburn
An Emilia Krekanyo Story
By Jack Harvey

Emilia was always nervous at this point. She'd been at the job for two weeks already but still got a case of the nerves every time she knocked at the door. That moment between the knock and the opening. Once the door was open, sure, she just had to rely on her script, sell the products. The worst that could happen was that they'd say no, and she'd move right along.

No, that wasn't quite true. The worst that could happen would be that *most* of them would say no. That she'd end the day with little to show and her daughters would have been deprived of her attention yet again. She hadn't wanted to work, but Jonathan, her husband, had insisted it was necessary. Wages were being cut at the factory, the old Ichabod Nickson was being edged out of the market by Masterforge Steel and Composites Limited, and it's bright young (for a dwarf) upstart Rune Masterforge.

"Never go into business against the dwarfs," Jonathan had been gratefully advised by his boss. "And most definitely never go into business against a woman."

So here she was, working door to door because her husband couldn't get the shifts. Letting her children be supervised by Suzi, her next door neighbour, who couldn't keep a cigarette out of her mouth for two minutes. Waiting nervously as though some terrible creature was lying in wait. Scared that it would open, even more scared that it would remain closed.

Finally the door did open, and a pleasant faced young woman greeted her.

"Hello," she beamed expectantly. She seemed more familiar to this than Emilia.

"Good afternoon," Emilia smiled back. "I'm here representing Axon cosmetics. I wonder if you would be interested in any of our make up, or maybe some of the fabulous perfumes we have on offer?"

***

The bullets spattered against the rocky surface Emilia was trying to use for cover. Gravel and dust blasted against her face. Dirt blackened her already dark skin. She closed her eyes tight, leaving herself open for ambush as she did. She knew it was a mistake, but couldn't help herself.

Mikkelson shouted something, and she opened her eyes again. She readied the heavy, unfamiliar rifle. They'd switched from bolt action to automatic over two months ago, but she still couldn't get a feel for the weapon, and they were notoriously unreliable.

"Another five coming from the left!" Mikkelson shouted, sliding up beside her. "Remember that we're not here to kill. We only need to buy time to let Winters finish the job." When Mikkelson spoke to Emilia, he patronized her a little, talked down to her, because she was a woman.

It wasn't just that, he treated Winters well enough, but because Winters kept her hair short and dressed like a tomboy, she was treated like one of the men. Emilia hadn't let go of her feminine side just yet. Though every battle took her closer to taking a knife to her hair.

The routine was supposed to be simple. Approach Vahandra, the great dragon, with care, and painlessly inject the creature with a non toxic solution. If poachers were to harvest the old one for it's blood, they wouldn't be able to hide. The solution contained an invisible die that would seep through the dragon's pores, that couldn't be washed off, and glowed when it came into contact with human flesh. It was an old DPS tactic. Over one hundred illegal poachers had been prosecuted over the last two decades because of it.

Yes, the Draconic Preservation Society. So proud they looked in their combat gear and white smocks emblazoned with the burning fist. Emilia hadn't been here long, but she struggled to remember what life was like before.

"Emilia began to fire. She didn't want to kill anybody. She didn't join for that. The poachers had given her little choice, however, and she wasn't about to let them take down another one of the aeons aged beasts."

Another crack of gunfire reminded her that there was no time for glory. Glory was for soldiers and politicians. The only reward a DPS member sought was seeing those majestic beasts take flight for one more day.

This time the poachers had second guessed them. Mikkelson didn't know who they were working for, but they'd grown tired of being hunted down and decided to take the fight to the DPS.

Emilia began to fire. She didn't want to kill anybody. She didn't join for that. The poachers had given her little choice, however, and she wasn't about to let them take down another one of the aeons old beasts.

****

"As you can see. Axon caters for all the major brands from the continent, as well as having an Avalonian selection for the more budget focused individual." Amilia prided herself on the phrasing of that last comment. It made it sound so much more sophisticated than referring to it as the cheap stuff made down the road. "And it's all at a lower price than your regular high street retailer."

"Well that looks wonderful," said the young woman, who had introduced herself as Mrs Rathbone. "I'm not sure though. My husband says that by buying direct from these companies, people will be putting the high street out of business."

This was a tricky one. Mrs Rathbone was right of course, and Emilia knew all too well the first hand affects of economic competition. Yet she needed the money, she didn't have the time nor the circumstance to care about the bigger picture. *So what if Axon put the high street stores out of business?* Emilia only cared about keeping food on the table and another month's mortgage paid.

"Well they do say that, but you must consider your own finances first Mrs Rathbone. A lady has to keep herself beautiful for her husband, whilst keeping the family fed too. You wouldn't want to end up in a situation where you'd have to choose between one or the other would you?"

Calculations resolved themselves in Mrs Rathbone's brain. Emilia prayed silently that her bogus logic would sound like sense.

"Well in that case," said Mrs Rathbone pulling out a pencil, despite the fact Emilia already had one ready. "I'll take the mascara and...

****

Emilia fired once, twice. No hits, but she was just trying to scare the poachers for now. They only needed to finish up with Vahandra, and the beast could defend itself. That was if it didn't turn on them too of course. Dragons could be notoriously indiscriminate.

The poachers were slowing now. Most of them lugged around crude shotguns and short ranged sub-machine guns. Their accuracy was patchy at best. Dragon poachers tended to spend most of their budget on ordinance, heat seeking missiles and hydrolic harpoons. Emilia pressed her attack before they could formulate a response. She fired a third time. A forth.

click

The rifle jammed. She dropped it to her knee, smacked it about a couple of times and returned to fire.

click

She cursed under her breath. She missed her old Enfield. They were slower than the new automatics, antiquated, but they did the job. These new weapons had been forced on them by their superiors. Most likely as a symbolic gesture to the millionaire philanthropists that they relied on for support. Visual proof that their donations were being put to good use. Alas, no good deed goes unpunished. The rifles were a liability at the best of times.

click

"Shit, fuck, bugger, tits!" Emilia spat. She swore in a tone that was unfamiliar to those words. Another thing her colleagues would tease her about.

She pulled out the magazine and tapped it hard three times against her blue helmet. She shook it to make sure any dust or grime wasn't clogging the rounds and slammed it back into place. Relived, she began firing again, for all the good it did. Most of the poachers were ignoring her and Mikkelson now.

They must have realised that Winters was up to something. A group of them had rallied, and charged deeper into the caverns. Emilia watched as they struggled up a mountain of rusted old coins that made up part of the Dragon's hoard.

****

Emilia had to stop herself from sighing in frustration when the door opened. The home-owner was an elf. Not that Emilia had anything against elves mind you, but they were a tough sell when it came to cosmetics. Elves were naturally beautiful, even the men, and though they tended to be very vain, it was not through disguising their flaws.

This one was no different. Tall, ethereal. She had golden hair down to her waist. Her deep blue eyes studied Emilia with confusion.

Emilia ran through her script, and the woman nodded and paid great attention to what she was saying. She made a little small talk with Emilia. She had a friendly smile all the while, and asked a few question about the products that were on sale. For a second, Emilia genuinely thought that the elf would buy something, but in the end just accepted a brochure and said she'd think about it. Not a complete fail, she might decide to buy something later by direct sales, and Emilia would get a cut of the capital, but she was probably just being polite.

The next door was a scruffy, overweight man who Emilia had apparently awoken from slumber. He insisted that he worked the night shift and that he was not unemployed. Emilia wondered why he thought she'd care. Ultimately he was unmarried and unaccounted for, so there was little interest in Axon's products for him.

Approaching the next house on the street, Emilia noticed a ragged cat looking out the window at her. It might have been her imagination, or her own feelings of entrapment, but she could have sworn that the creature was silently begging for rescue. The windows were fogged up with grime, and the front lawn a mess of mud and weeds.

She knocked at the door, and an older woman greeted her quickly, cigarette in mouth. It immediately reminding Emilia of Suzi supervising her children. A painful reminder of her priorities. Maybe the woman wasn't as old as she thought, maybe her cavernous face was down to the ravages of nicotine and drink.

“Good afternoon, I'm here representing Axon cosmetics. I wonder if you would be interested in any of our make up, or maybe some of the fabulous perfumes we have on offer.” *Blah blah blah,* Emilia thought, and no doubt the woman did too, as she ran through her script. The woman accepted the brochure, cigarette still in hand, ashes burning little specks into the pages.

“An' you use these products do you, duck?” the woman asked.

“I do.” Emilia nodded and smiled. “I can personally guarantee their quality.”

“Well that don't do a lotta' good for me do it? I'm not a Golden Lander.”

Emilia bit her tongue. She wanted to tell the lady about how she was a third generation Avalonian. That she'd never set foot on the southern continent. That wasn't quite what the lady was saying though was it? Emilia's skin was dark, and her’s was pale. It was a reasonable enough question, but it caught her off guard. Emilia was smart though. Smart and quick.

“Actually our brochure has a skin tone chart at the back. Do you see?” The woman turned the pages over with her yellow stained fingers. “Each foundation has a rating, one though to twelve. Also, a D1 for those specifically tailored for dark elves.” The charts were never really as useful as Emilia made out, but felt there was no harm in exaggerating her own expertise.

“Fucking fruits.” The woman said, unprompted. “You don't want to be selling anything to their kind.”

*"She knocked at the door,
and an older woman greeted her quickly. She had a
cigarette in her mouth, immediately reminding Emilia
of Suzi supervising her children right this moment."*

Emilia glanced over at the cat at the window. Fear radiated from it's frayed hide. Emilia could stand cruelty between people, just, but she could never stand cruelty to animals. If it wasn't for the fact that she needed the money, she'd have grabbed the brochure out of the woman's hand and left that instant.

"Put me down for some of that foundation, duck. The seventy five."

****

It was the Orc that charged at her. Somehow it was always Orcs that found themselves associating with undesirables, but they were never the ones calling the shots. For some reason his comrades had left him with only a rusted old battle axe, or maybe he had chosen it himself. Either way, Emilia and Mikkelson marched carefully forward, metal coins crunching between their feet. Emilia made a mental note to maybe grab something pretty from the dragon's horde to give to her daughters next time she saw them.

They both popped off rounds at the warrior as he got nearer.

"Don't restrain yourself," Mikkelson said again in that same condescending tone. "If you get the chance to put them down, do it. We're in a life or death situation here."

Their enemy was still about twenty yards away. Emilia fired a few more rounds, one of which hit the Orc in the leg. Mikkelson took the opportunity to hit him with two in the chest and the Orc fell to the ground.

Emilia shook her head, just slightly.

"Hey," Mikkelson put a hand on her shoulder, "Keep it together, we've got to stop them getting to Winters."

Members of the DPS were not soldiers, they had no real rank or discipline. They were just a bunch of volunteers with some basic training and guns in their hands. In the end that was all they needed to be. The poachers they fought, mostly, were desperate poor men drawn to the hunting of dragons to make ends meet, or street level thugs trying to make names for themselves. The two sides were more similar than they liked to admit.

Suddenly Mikkelson jerked, and looked to the ground. He had stepped over one of their own fallen brethren, a halfling named Goldie Jambottom, a farmer's son. He had taken a round through the cheek. Now he was with Saxon Bumblebee, god of the Halflings.

More gunshot sounds came from the caves above. Emilia and Mikkelson ran for the breach but struggled to hold their footing on the mound of coins. One upon a time this would have been an adventurer's dream, now it was a conservationist's nightmare.

****

Emilia had been demoralized by the previous home-owner, despite the fact she had secured a sale. She longed for the end of the road when she could call it a day, go home and see her children again.

She knocked on the door, and was a little taken aback to find that a short goblin creature, dressed in an apron, greeted her. For a moment she thought it was maybe some kind of servant, a cleaner maybe.

"Wot?" the creature said in a voice that sounded like an old crone. It's large eyes squinted past it's long arched nose. *Her* eyes, Emilia reminded herself. The goblin was a woman after all.

Emilia smiled and started her speech once again. It was unusual to find a goblin owning a home this side of the city. Many lived in poverty, but then again, she reminded herself, a run of bad luck could put anyone on the wrong side of the tracks.

"Make up?" the goblin said, a slight grin across her face. "You think that'd be a good idea."

Emilia paused. She didn't know what to say. A goblin's face was about as far from conventionally attractive as one could get. Putting make up on would be like trying to stop a fire with a tablespoon of water. Then Emilia kicked herself, she was in no position to judge. The last thing she wanted was to be compared to the horrible woman next door.

“Our products are designed to appeal to a wide range of customers. I'm sure there's something we have that would catch you eye.”

A couple of goblin children ran into the hallway. They were tiny, spindly things, with nothing but bony legs and arms. “What's the human lady want mummy?” one said. “Chocolates, Chocolates,” chanted the other, pulling on the mothers apron.

“Bugger off you two, go back in the room,” she waved them off. “Go back to playing with your blocks.”

“Lovely children,” Emilia said cheerfully, half lying. “I have two just like them?”

“How much cheaper?” the goblin woman asked sharply.

“I'm sorry?”

“How much cheaper is this stuff compared to the high street?” the woman pointed at the brochure.

“Oh,” Emilia jumped, her salesmanship returning. “Well if you order from me today, you can get as much as twenty five to thirty percent off retail price.”

She nodded, and thought about it. “Fuck it, put me down for a bottle of Flannel Number 5”

****

Emilia was short of breath. For a second she thought Mikkelson was going to scold her for slowing down, but he was too. Reaching the top of the mound of coins, they were dismayed to see another one, just as high, reaching further into the caves. Winters was nowhere to be seen.

"Shit, Krekanyo, down." Mikkelson shouted with what little breath he still had. They noticed the other three poachers they had exchanged bullets with earlier. The two of them dived behind a wooden chest as bullets bounced off coins and old candlesticks.

Mikkelson popped up, fired. His gun jammed, but he tried again. Still nothing, the men were getting closer. Emilia reached over to help. "Here," she said, reaching for the magazine, but Mikkelson, in his arrogance, pulled the trigger again.

The rifle backfired, it's mechanism shattered and a fragment of metal flew past Emilia's cheek, slicing into her flesh. Mikkelson put his arm over his eyes, possibly blinded.

Emilia threw her rifle to the ground in frustration. Shouting in rage, she pulled two pistols out of her back holsters and turned towards the poachers. She got all the way up, making an easy target out of herself, but before the poachers could take advantage she blazed away with the pistols. Every shot rang true, and the attackers all dropped to the floor, scattering coins beneath their bodies. It was over.

"Not bad," Mikkelson coughed, "for a girl."

Emilia smiled, thoughts longing for her husband, and helped Mikkelson to his feet.

"I can only hope Sarah managed to hold them off on her end." Emilia whispered, mouth dry with dirt.

Prophetically, they heard a rapid crunching of feet on coins above them. "Heyyyy!!!" came a gravelly, but clearly femininity shout.

"Speak of the devils," said Mikkelson.

"Get fucking moving, big red's all done and she's pissed as all hell." Winters came sliding down the pile of coins at break neck speed, her shortish hair blown back straight. The stylist in Emilia thought she should keep it that way.

The three of them ran and began to slide down the next slope of coins, as they heard an incandescent roar from behind them. Emilia looked back briefly, to see the majestic dragon spread it's leathery wings and glide out of the cavern. Words could not describe the creatures, their flesh shimmered purple and green, their scales like chrome and oil.

Vahandra flew out of the cave, snaking through the air towards the encampment of poachers Emilia could see in the distance. They tried to ready their rocket launcher, but Goldie had already sabotaged it earlier. The dragon gasped, though it was more of a scream, readying to release it's fiery breath.

She could bet they knew they were fucked. Moment's later, nothing remained but the charred husk of the vehicles, and Vahandra making gains for the horizon.

“Yes, yeah, boom, boom, fucking boom, boom, boom, boom.” Winters chanted as she and Mikkelson fist bumped.

Emilia herself was in a daze, on the way down she had snagged a small locket. She held it in her hand and examined it. The pictures inside were faded, but she felt it would be a nice trinket to put photos of her daughters in. The wound in her cheek stung, and she leaned back and looked into the sky.

****

Another sale. Emilia couldn't complain. One more house and the day was done, she could count her gains and losses later. She knocked at the door and was greeted by a friendly looking older woman. She smiled.

“Good afternoon, I'm here representing Axon cosmetics. I wonder if you would be interested in any of our make up...”

Halfway through her speech, a group of five of six friendly looking dogs came running to their masters feet, yapping in greeting to Emilia. She couldn't help herself, and started laughing.

*"The dragon gasped, though it
was more of a scream, readying to release it's fiery breath.
Moment's later nothing remained but the fiery husk of the vehicles,
and Vahandra flew off towards the horizon.."*

"Oh, I'm sorry. It's been such a long day." Emilia said, apologetically through her smile. "Your dogs are so adorable."

The woman picked up two of them, a poodle and a whippet, "I love my babies," she said with pride. "I love all animals. I would have more if I could fit them in the house."

"I adore them too," Emilia said. "I can't stand cruelty. I couldn't believe what I saw in that woman's window up the street."

"Mrs Chatnow is a savage," the woman nodded in agreement. She took a better look at Emilia. "But oh, my dear, you look exhausted. Have you been on your feet all day?"

"Five hours," Emilia said honestly.

"Oh do come in, take the weight off your feet, let me make you a cuppa," the woman said, putting the dogs back down, they yapped happily in unison and Emilia didn't stand on ceremony.

"Emily is the name," the woman said.

"Emilia."

"Oh our names are so similar, how about that?" Emily said as she shut the door behind her.

Emilia looked at a nearby table in the hallway. It was littered with framed pictures of dogs, along with a leaflet for some kind of animal charity or other. Emilia picked it up. Emily returned with a cup of tea.

"Sugar?"

"No thank you."

Emily noticed that Emilia had picked up the leaflet. "My husband and I are active contributors to the fight against animal cruelty. You wouldn't even begin to imagine the things going on around the realms. Do you donate?"

"I've always wanted to," Emilia said, "but I'd never really found time to think about it. To be honest we're strapped for cash as it is. I'm working door to door because my husband can't get the shifts."

Emily smiled gently. "I understand, but there are other ways one can contribute to the cause. It is a rewarding purpose to dedicate one's life to." She put her hand gently over Emilia's shoulder. "Come into the living room dear, and I'll tell you all about it."

NEW · REGIME · PRESS · FICTION ·
NR
£0.46
Free!
Tales of the Modern Realms
HOPE NEVER SLEEPS
A Quentin Wilde Story
By Jack Harvey
JH2014

Tales of the Modern Realms
Hope Never Sleeps
A Quentin Wilde Story
By Jack Harvey

Dawn had broken over Gulf City. Such was it's beauty that this very country had been christened after it, New Dawn. Quentin rose, stretching his arms. He sighed. He wasn't as young as he used to be. A crack of light had found it's way through the curtains. Through his drowsy eyes it reminded him of a flaming sword. He smiled at the thought of that.

He felt hands running over the contours of his back. Over muscle that still looked pretty defined for a man his age. The hands were shortly followed by kisses from a mouth that slowly ran over to his neck.

"Why so early?" the young man said.

"Why not?" Quentin had responded cheerfully. "The day is so full of potential. Why waste it by lying around in bed?"

"Well, it's not wasted if you're lying around in bed *with* someone." The man moved his arms around Quentin's side and over his chest.

Quentin grinned and put his own hands over them. He caressed them gently, before pulling them away. Much to the young man's disappointment he rose and walked to the nearby wardrobe to retrieve his clothes.

"Aww," the man sighed.

Quentin fastened his shirt and began to straighten his magnificent handlebar moustache. Quentin gave a brief laugh. Most of the men he'd known were only in it for the money. An opportunity for some old queer, show biz has-been to pay for their food and drinks for the night. They seemed to think all they had to do in return was make an old man feel like he was twenty-two again. Quentin had seen it so many times he had developed a sixth sense. He avoided them like the plague.

Not like this young man though, this Dean Hanson. He was genuinely star struck when his eyes first fell upon the Avalonian singer. The two had hit it off from the get go, Dean's intense knowledge of the music industry made for fascinating conversation, and he didn't bore Quentin with the usual questions fans had asked one million times before.

And he was honest, a virtue Quentin valued above all else. Dean made no attempt to hide what he wanted, and Quentin was glad that he didn't have to either.

"Get up," Quentin slapped Dean's shoulder playfully. "Life isn't a fairy tale."

"Awww." Dean groaned again. "Fine. I can use your shower right?"

"Well I'm hardly going to say no am I?" Quentin responded, picking up the newspaper that had been slipped under the door.

***

Room service had brought up breakfast. Quentin slipped the server a wad of notes as a 'tip'. He was a large Orc by the name of Grobnar, whom many would presume would be too dumb to conclude why Dean was even there, but Quentin had learned long ago never to underestimate Orcs. If you showed them loyalty then they would reciprocate in kind.

It was over scrambled eggs that Dean surprised Quentin with a question.

"You ever been in love Quentin?" he asked, casually.

Quentin paused for a moment. Cleared his throat. "What makes you ask?" he responded, a slight tremble in his voice.

"Just curious. It's hard finding someone when it comes to... people of our persuasion."

"Once," Quentin nodded. "A long time ago."

"That was back in Avalon right? During your time in the national service?"

Quentin smiled evasively. "Close enough. What about you?"

"A guy back home in Mithrilham." Dean began. "We were at school together."

"What happened?" Quentin asked.

"Nothing."

"Then where is he now?"

Dean laughed. "What was I supposed to do? Shack up with him? He was dependant on taking over his pop's repair shop. If he had found out... and me, I flunked every class in school, what was I supposed to offer him?"

"And so you came to Gulf City. To make your fortune I imagine. I've heard that before." Quentin didn't intend to sound condescending, but he was staunchly against sugar coating the truth as a rule.

"That wasn't it," said Dean defensively. "I just... I knew Gulf City was somewhere where someone like me could just bleed into the background. There's a lot of big faces, someone like me won't draw attention to themselves."

Quentin took a sip of tea. He nodded again and smiled. "I understand."

They finished breakfast in silence before parting ways. Quentin knew better than to offer Dean money. It would dirty their relationship, make it feel wrong. Dean probably would have refused anyway. Quentin said he would call him in due course. Any messages could be left with Carol the hotel receptionist.

Alone now, Quentin went to his clothes drawer to pick out his tie for the day. *Maybe the red silk? No, the navy blue would be better.* He was meeting the legendary Thomas Bygraves later, and Thomas always complained about Quentin's colourful ties.

Then again, he was in the mood for winding Thomas up.

He heard a sound from over by the door. A sweeping brush. It took him a moment to see that something had been slipped under the door. *Strange*, he thought. The papers had already been delivered. He walked over. It was a large brown envelope.

He seethed with rage. He wanted to tear it up, to burn it all, but knew that wouldn't solve anything. The envelope contained a note, a time, a place of meeting.

Thomas Bygraves would have to wait.

"The young man was sitting in the booth at the end of the room.
He dressed smart, but was an ill fit for his suit and tie.
He had sickly yellowing skin, possibly earth born,
or maybe he just had a bad complexion."

The diner was a scruffy little place on the outskirts of the city. It wasn't bad by any means but there was a reason Quentin never set foot in a place like this. He dressed down in a boring brown coat. His mysterious adversary had wanted to keep things low key, so the last thing he wanted was people hassling him for autographs.

Gaudy pop music played on the jukebox. Some bubblegum-sweet nonsense by a singer barely old enough to string together a tune. It was also a painful reminder that artists like he and Thomas' days were numbered. One could only be in the limelight for so long.

The young man was sitting in the booth at the end of the room. He dressed smart, but was an ill fit for his suit and tie. He had sickly yellowing skin, possibly earth born, or maybe he just had a bad complexion. His nose arched like the beak of an angry eagle. His hair could have used a stylist or two.

Quentin sat. He slapped down the heavy envelope.

"You found the place alright then?" The man said, fidgeting nervously. He spoke with faux concern, a tremble in his voice half way between fear and arrogance. "Don't expect a big shot like you would frequent a place like this."

Quentin was about to get down to business, but they were suddenly interrupted by a hostess.

"Can I get you guys anything?" she said, a smile beaming from her face.

"Coffee, black." The man said.

"Tea please. Hot if you would." Responded Quentin without looking at her. "Milk. One sugar."

"Can I get you anything to eat? Pie maybe?"

"No thank you." The two men said in unison.

"Oh-kay" Said the server, a little weirded out. "I'll be right back."

There was silence for a moment. The man had a subtle but clearly vindictive grin on his face.

Quentin didn't wait for introductions. "Look, let's not beat around the bush here. You have pictures of me in a compromising position. To be frank I honestly don't care if you plaster my naked body all over the city, but this young man doesn't deserve to be dragged into it. For his sake, and his alone is my only reason to be here."

"What makes you think he wasn't in on it?" The man asked. "What makes you think we hadn't set this whole thing up together?"

Quentin retrieved a cigarette and it's holder. He lit it, and balanced the holder between his lips casually. "I had considered that, but no. I've had enough men pretend in an attempt to get something out of me. I'd have seen it a mile away. Besides, if he was, you would have either told me, or not brought it up. Instead you posited that ridiculous question, which only goes to prove that he's not part of the equation."

The man was clearly discomforted by Quentin's confidence. He had probably hoped that Quentin would come grovelling. A shamed beast. Instead he could tell he was just a beat away from losing his chance. It was the best way Quentin thought. Make your terms clear from the get go. Put them on the back foot. You want to make them do the negotiations, not the other way around.

"Listen old man, you can pretend you don't care, but if this gets to the press then your career is over. You think your audience of screaming girls is gonna' stick around when they find out you're a fag?"

Quentin didn't say anything at first, instead breathing out a steady stream of smoke. "They call cigarettes fags back home you know?"

The man shook his head in confusion, failing to understand Quentin's non sequitur.

The hostess brought over their drinks. Only Quentin gave her thanks. He could tell she knew who he was, but she didn't say anything, likely in fear of the intense frustration that was radiating from the other man now.

"What is it you want?" Quentin simply asked.

"Five million."

Quentin giggles softly, much to his host's chagrin. “I don't have five million.”

“Then find it.”

Quentin laughed fully this time. “What am I supposed to do? Rob a bank?”

“I don't know. Ask some of your showbiz friends, they can front it for you.” The man was growing impatient now. His fidgeting was getting worse, and there was a thin layer of sweat developing on his forehead. “I know you're pally with that Thomas Bygraves.”

“He's practically bankrupt. I think you've chosen the wrong mark here my dear chap.”

He man slammed his hand on the table. Onlookers glanced over. “Look, I don't care what you do, or how you get it. You don't want these pictures leaked, you wouldn't have come here if you did. Maybe it doesn't matter to you if your fans find out what you really are but It'll be embarrassing all the same.”

“What I really am?” Quentin mirrored, his smile leaving his face “You have no idea what I am dear boy.”

“Just get the money,” the man stood. “Be here tomorrow, with at least half, preferably all.” He began to walk away, before he suddenly paused. “You can pick up the tab.”

Quentin took out his wallet and dropped a few notes on the table as payment. The man must have thought he'd somehow gotten the last word. He waited patiently for his blackmailer to disappear out of sight.

Once he was sure the man had gone Quentin stood and gazed out the window. An inconspicuous black car pulled into view, a stones throw away from the entrance. The driver side window wound down. A sinister looking, blue-skinned lizard man in a fedora looked over at Quentin. Without a word of response he nodded, then wound up the window and drove away.

Quentin walked over to a payphone that was near the table and pushed in a few coins.

"Operator," a voice responded.

"The Blitmoor Hotel please."

"Connecting you."

"Carol. It's me. Just letting you know that Sidnar's going to be dropping by with some information for me. Have it ready when I get back from a few drinks with Thomas."

"Sure thing Mr Wilde," the receptionist said pleasantly. "Is it blackmail again?"

"It is. I don't know what it is about this time of year. Maybe they're all getting their tax returns in and finding out they had a bigger bill than usual." He sighed.

"I'll have it all ready for you when you get here. Anything else?"

"Make sure my laundry is picked up from the dry cleaners," she said.

"I'll let Grobnar know. It'll be folded and in your room when you get back."

"Thanks Carol. See you in a bit."

"See you later Mr Wilde."

Quentin put the phone down and made to leave. On his way out, the hostess that had been serving them smiled. He smiled back.

"You're him aren't you?" she asked.

"I am," he said. "Autograph?"

***

Quentin had returned to the hotel by late afternoon. He was a little light headed due to one too many cocktails with his old friend Thomas. In an optimistic mood, he approached Carol at reception, his sharp heels clicking on the marble floor. Good, he thought, her colleagues had all clocked off. They could speak with privacy.

"Afternoon Mr Wilde," she said cordially.

"Carol," Quentin nodded, "You have something for me?"

She ducked under the oversized desk. Half way down, Quentin stopped her.

"It's alright Carol, you might as well just tell me. I know you read through all of my messages."

"Oh, Mr Wilde," she said, panicked. "It's not like that I just..."

"It's alright," he repeated and leaned forward to slip some notes into her blazer pocket. "I trust you. What is it that Sidnar found out?"

Carol looked around to make sure there were no eavesdroppers. She then leaned forward and lowered her voice. "His name is Michael Herbert. Lives out on the east side. Apparently he's no stranger to schemes like this. He regularly hits the strip to try and catch big names in embarrassing situations. He's made a little money off of it but never really had a big payday. Don't know what drew him to you Mr Wilde."

"Could have just been instinct or luck I suppose," Quentin pondered. "You have an address?"

She handed the message from Sidnar over. "Mr Tlaloc will be picking you up at Eleven Mr Wilde. Will that be sufficient?"

"Perfectly," Quentin said, smiling. "I take it Sidnar is confident Mr Herbert will be home at the time?"

"That seems likely."

"Good. My laundry is ready?"

"Waiting for you in your room." Carol said, a professional tone returned to her voice.

"Good," Quentin leaned forwards and put a friendly hand on her shoulder. "Thanks Carol, I don't know what I'd do without you."

"Thank you Mr Wilde." She blushed.

Quentin smiled and proceeded to walk to the elevators.

"Quentin looked at himself in the mirror, reminding himself that there was a reason he couldn't wear the robes in public any more. It was a shame."

The robe was waiting for him in his room. It was folded amongst shirts and jumpers, and other formal wear. Inconspicuous. Nobody at the laundrette would give it a second thought. That was intentional. It was not in the robe's nature to draw attention to itself.

Calmly, Quentin loosened his tie. Undone his shirt and dropped his trousers. He switched his underwear for a pair of long-johns. The robes were loose, could get draughty, and Gulf City was hardly warm this time of year.

There was magic in the fabric, that was the robe's secret. Once, long ago, the realms had wondered why Quentin's people were as powerful as they were. The secret was that a person could only hold so much sway over magic. The brain and the heart could only handle so much power. Fabric, however, could be weaved with power ten times that a man could handle. It was like a battery, in a way, charging up the user with the power of three thousand suns.

As soon as he slipped them on he could feel that power. It was subtle, but noticeable. It were as though he had just been hit with ten espressos, or jumped into a pool of ice cold water. It was a wake up call.

Quentin looked at himself in the mirror, reminding himself that there was a reason he couldn't wear the robes in public any more. It was a shame.

Quietly, he chanted. "Invisibilium."

He slipped out of the door, nary casting a shadow. Sidnar would know where to find him.

***

Sidnar's eyes lingered on Quentin as he made his way towards the car. Quentin had been a valued customer after all these years, but even for a private eye he knew so little about him. There were many questions Sidnar wanted to ask, but knew it was more than his job's worth to try.

Quentin looked different when he wore the robes. There was a wrongness about him, but also a clarity. Sidnar once said it was like he had been painted by oils when all the realm was watercolour.

"Is he in?" Quentin asked from the passenger seat.

"He is," the lizardman said in a gravelly voice, opening the car door and returning to the driver's seat. "Apartment 104."

"Well then. I suppose I'd better get this over with," Quentin said wearily.

"Are you sure you don't want me to be there?" Sidnar asked, pulling out a snub-nosed revolver. "For backup."

"Not necessary, as you well know." Quentin opened the car door and made to exit. "I appreciate the sentiment, but the less you know, the less you have to worry about old friend."

"As you wish."

"I'm sure you need no reminding," Quentin said, handing over a wad of notes wrapped in a brown paper bag. "This did not happen. I was not here."

Sidnar nodded without comment and pocketed the payment.

Quentin turned towards the run down apartment block. Faded lights glowed a bilious orange through it's dirty curtains. Apparently Michael Herbert had accrued numerous gambling debts and was looking for an easy way for some fast cash. He'd gotten greedy.

Quentin played back the day's events in his mind. He wondered, in actual fact, if it wasn't just pride that prevented him from paying up. After all, money had already changed hands between Grobnar, Carol and Sidnar. *Was paying for their own silence really that much different? Would they show the same loyalty if he didn't have a penny to his name?*

These were questions for another time, Quentin concluded. It wasn't just his own good name that was at stake here. In the cool twilight hours he glided across the street, his long robe dragging itself through cigarette butts and oil stains.

He slid through the door, ascended the stairs without making a sound, and quickly located Herbert's room. The door had scratches on it, from the claws of a dog most likely. One of the numbers was snapped in half.

He was still tough for a man of his age. Quentin could have kicked down the door if he wanted to, but these days he preferred the subtle approach. Slowly he hovered his hand over the door handle.

"Aperio."

The lock clicked and he slid it open silently.

The room was still dim but slightly illuminated. Old film posters peeled off the walls and a layer of dust gave the whole place the feeling of a crypt. The furniture was brown and stained with nicotine. Empty bottles of beer mingled with showbiz gossip magazines. Herbert liked to do his research in his off hours it would appear.

Herbert himself was passed out on a recliner. It was the cleanest piece of furniture in the room. Quentin was greeted with an unfortunate view of Herbert's yellowing teeth.

Time to end this. Quentin grabbed Herbert by the collar, shaking him awake. The young man was confused at first, but then his eyes widened once he recognised Quentin.

"Hello Michael," Quentin smiled in mock sincerity.

Herbert wasn't given time to formulate a response. With superhuman strength Quentin picked him up and threw him across the room.

Herbert crashed face first into a mostly empty bookcase. His nose broke and his skin split. Blood gushed out of his battered face. That wasn't yet enough for Quentin though. He grabbed Herbert again and began punching him, using good old fashioned brawn this time.

Herbert pushed him away with surprising strength, and made to run across the room. Quentin threw forward an outstretched hand. Three blades materialised and pinned Herbert to the wall. The young man was quick though, and didn't panic. He ripped his shirt and trousers to free himself and ran for a nearby desk.

"Herbert wasn't given time to formulate a response. With superhuman strength Quentin picked him up and threw him across the room."

Quentin was readying another torrent of torments when he noticed Herbert pull out a gun. To his relief, the man didn't fire.

"Yeah," the bloody Michael Herbert said, rising to his feet. "You don't like fucking guns do you? Fucking spell casters. Think you can beat the truth out of me? I ain't telling you where those pictures are. They're fucking going to the press after this bullshit."

"My dear boy, I'm not worried about the pictures," Quentin raised his hand defensively in an effort to placate Herbert's trigger finger. "This isn't an interrogation."

He thrust one of his hands forwards and pain shot though Herbert's body. The man winced in agony. Quentin thrust his second hand forwards and Herbert's gun rusted and dissolved into dust.

He lunged at Herbert, punched him twice and then threw him into the nearby bathroom. Herbert fell to his hands and knees. Quentin grabbed Herbert and smacked his skull against the toilet. To add insult to injury, he shoved Herbert's head into the bowl and flushed.

Once Herbert had stopped struggling Quentin finally let him go. Calmly, Quentin rose to his feet and took out his cigarette holder, lighting a fresh one up. He took smooth slow breaths of it as Herbert gasped desperately for air.

"If you kill me you'll never find those pictures!" He shot, still full of rage and hatred.

Quentin smirked. "My people already have the pictures. A safety deposit box at Lincoln station. All the smutty little peepers like you use them."

Herbert's arms sloped to his side in defeat.

"Like I said, this wasn't an interrogation. It's not a silencing either. Giving you a good hiding was just for my own personal satisfaction."

"Turn you on does it faggot?" Herbert said, in one final attempt at retaliation.

Quentin shook his head. As if everything he did somehow had to come back to sex. “My dear boy, what I get up to in the privacy of my own home is far from the greatest secret I hide. Funny that you should get so close to it and be denied.” He contemplated giving Herbert another beating for his troubles, but that would have been a little excessive. Quentin pulled his now used cigarette out of it's holder and stubbed it out in the bathroom's sink.

“What the fuck does that mean?” Herbert asked.

Quentin put his palm over the man's eyes, and chanted softly.“Oblivisci.”

Herbert slipped out of consciousness. He lay by the toilet for only a brief moment. When he opened his eyes again he looked around at the chaos in the room. Confused, he looked up at Quentin. He didn't recognise the man.

“Hello my dear chap. Are you alight?” Quentin said with concern.

Herbert still didn't say anything at first. He looked around again. “Where am I? Who are you?”

“You're home.” Quentin said in a comforting tone. He put a friendly hand on Herbert's arm “I'm just a concerned citizen who found you a little worse for wear after one too many drinks.”

“Fuck I feel terrible. Is this blood?”

“You got into a fight with a few vagrants. That's when I found you. I managed to warn them off and helped you get home. You made a bit of a mess as you can see.” Quentin waved an arm at the main room. “Brought you in here to clean yourself up and you passed out on the floor.”

“Fuck that must have been one hell of a night.” Herbert looked around in confusion once again. “Could you believe I can't remember a thing?”

“Believe me,” Quentin said, “from what I've seen you wouldn't want to remember it.”

***

Quentin had called for Dean two days later. It was the earliest he could permit it as he and Thomas Bygraves had had business out of town to attend to. He asked that they meet in the hotel car park instead of the usual place. Dean sounded worried, but Quentin assured him it was nothing to be concerned about. Quentin waited for about half an hour for him to show.

"Dean," Quentin nodded, forgoing the usual formalities. "I take it you have an inkling as to what this is about?"

"I do," he said, a little upset. "This is it isn't it? The goodbye."

"Dean," He put his hand on the young man's shoulder as he had done to so many over the last few days. "I will always value the time we spent together, truly, but things like this were never meant to last forever. You told me you were in love once. I can't get in the way of that."

"I told you that was never going to happen," Dean said.

"Maybe not but..." Quentin pulled out a brown paper bag, it was obvious what it contained.

"Oh no," Dean shook his head sharply, offended. "You're not going to buy me off. No way." He pushed away Quentin's arm.

"I'm not buying you off Dean. Call it a parting gift. Events in this world are moving faster than I anticipated. I'll be leaving Gulf City soon. You should too."

"What am I supposed to do?"

"I don't know," Quentin shrugged "Buy your friend's father's garage. Be a silent partner. There's enough in here that you'd never have to worry about supporting yourselves."

Dean shook his head aggressively. "People would figure something was up."

"Maybe. But you won't have to hide forever Dean. The realms are changing, and they're changing quicker than some people realize. Soon a day will come where people like us won't have to hide at all."

"How can you think that?" Dean asked, sceptical at Quentin's optimism.

"Because I'm old Dean. I've seen history unfold, and the one thing I've learned from watching is that hate is a finite resource. It can only burn for so long until it runs out of fuel, but more often than not the rain will just wash it all away."

Dean couldn't quite understand the intricacies of what Quentin was getting at, but he could understand the importance of what he was saying. Dean begrudgingly accepted the money.

They hugged affectionately for the final time and didn't say a further word. As he left, Dean looked over his shoulder a few times, perhaps wondering if Quentin would change his mind.

Quentin didn't. Instead he unlocked the door to his roadster, and put the keys in the ignition. He wasn't lying, the realms really were changing, and he couldn't sit on the sidelines any longer. He put his foot to the peddle, and got ready to drive off into what he hoped was the beginning of a new world.

Tales of the Modern Realms
NEW · REGIME · PRESS · FICTION ·
NR
~~£0.46~~
Free!
THE FLAGS OF CASTOR ISLAND
A Gravis Grayslate Story
By Jack Harvey
JH2015

Tales of the Modern Realms
The Flags of Castor Island
A Gravis Grayslate Story
By Jack Harvey

"The flags," Gravis said, somewhat mystified. "They look as though they could have been made yesterday."

"And yet they were strung up centuries ago," came a guff voice off to his right. It was the Orc, Thorof.

"I detect no magic." Gravis said, still looking at the flags in wonder.

Thorof nodded, before quickly returning to help Blessed tie up the boat.

The crisp, triangular, blue and white flags, held aloft on a long cord, flapped in the wind. Gravis' eyes followed the line up, watching as it disappeared into the mists.

"Interesting isn't it?" boomed a commanding voice behind him. "They say that the mountain was used for funeral processions. That the Aether would march to the top of the mountain like a pilgrimage and watch below as hundreds of burning ships would take their dead to the heavens.

Gravis nodded, though he knew most of the myths already.

Castor Island was a picaresque rock on the northern coast of Avalon. It was not difficult to get to, but the government had classified it as off limits. The island was predominantly a narrow mountain, hundreds of leagues tall, it's summit theorised to once have been a ceremonial site for the long dead Aether civilisation. Few had been able to decipher the island's mysteries, even in these enlightened times.

Many had scaled the mountain, and many had reached the top, but none had come back down with anything save the vaguest of information. Most returned amnesic, with little memory of that which had unfolded. Others would return with their minds fractured, driven insane. What caused this phenomena none could say.

Still men came, some to brag and some for answers. Legend had it that the peak lies on the borders between the realms and the heavens, and if one can scale the foggy cliffs they would be rewarded with answers to life's greatest mysteries.

Sometimes the lonely or the desperate are willing to take the risks.

That is what brought these three men here. First was Michael “Blessed” DeMonfort, a popular dwarvern travel writer best known for scaling the mountains of both The Everwinter and The Spine.

The other two men kept their motivations closer to their chests. Thorof Teethsmasher, an unexpectedly intelligent Orc from a family of nine siblings. He was the only one not to follow them into the mercenary business. Finally, Gravis Grayslate, a dark elf, from a culture often ostracised for their hedonistic ways. Even with their eccentric personalities, he would be seen as a strange bedfellow.

Gravis had kept to himself for the journey by boat however, and Blessed was willing to accept help from anyone who'd scale the mountain with him. The elf pulled out a revolver from his waistcoat and checked the loaded cylinder casually.

“Oh, no, no, no, no, no, no, no, no, no!” Blessed came striding over, a fatherly tone to his voice. “We shall not be taking weapons with us Mr Grayslate.”

“Are you that confident for our safety Mr DeMonfrot?” Gravis looked down at the dwarf.

“Quite the contrary Sir. Castor Island houses no native life that would be hostile to us, but it is well known that the journey can put great strain on the psyche. The last thing I want is someone pulling out a weapon in the heat of an argument.” He nodded to the boat. “Tie it with the rest of the gear. It will be quite safe.”

Gravis had no cause to cross his comrades this early in their endeavour, so he did as he was commanded. As a dark elf he was also adept in the powers of death magic. He silently hoped that he wouldn't be called to rely on it.

“And another thing,” said Blessed, “Are you sure you wish to make the journey in that... attire? It is an overnight trip sir.”

Blessed was referring to the fact that while he and Thorof had dressed accordingly for a two day hike, Gravis had still insisted on coming in his best waistcoat and slacks. Mercifully he had brought the appropriate boots and coat, but it was still far from ideal.

"He'll manage," said Thorof, "won't you Gravis?"

The Orc was behaving oddly familiar for a man who had barely since they met. Gravis nodded all the same. "I will," he said pulling a cigarette from a silver case, and offering one to the others. Thorof partook, Blessed didn't.

Before long they had secured their packs, and began marching along the mossy flat ground towards the mountain's incline. The flags still flapped uncaring in the wind.

****

Gravis' pants chafed against his legs as he strode uphill, his skin burning into the fabric. Though he was over one hundred and fifty years the dwarf's senior, he tried not to let pride get the better of him when the stocky dwarf strode ahead once more. In an effort to slow him down, Gravis decided to strike up a conversation, which he valiantly tried to dictate whilst panting for air.

"You've scaled The Spine," he said as he gasped. "A far greater height than this. Wasn't that enough? Why this? Why now?"

Blessed smiled, he could tell what Gravis was doing. He sat on a rock to let the elf catch his breath. "It had to be done," he shrugged. "My readers want to know. They want to know, at the very least, what is at the top of Castor Island." He beat his chest. It was a hard knock indicating the journal he kept in his jacket. "Whatever happens, even if this journey drives me mad, I shall at least have something written down."

Blessed pulled open a skin of water and took a sip, then offered it to Gravis. He was grateful despite his slower metabolism.

Thorof looked off into the fog, ignoring Blessed's chatter as tough he'd heard it all before.

"And what about the authorities?" Gravis asked. "Us being here isn't strictly legal you know?"

"Pish posh!" Blessed waved a stubby arm. "A trespassing charge at best. A man of my calibre, they'll just slap me with a fine. They'd probably even waver it, after all, if this gets published it'll deter the curious from coming over here themselves."

Gravis nodded again. Oddly he started to feel as though he were the student in this relationship.

Blessed slapped his knee. "Now come on, we've only just begun. Rest too long and your legs will seize up. The journey will be all the harder."

With that the two men rose to their feet. Blood rushed to their heads, and they began to charge onward.

****

Thanks to the oncoming fog the grassy ground underfoot was wet and muddy. Visibility had decreased since the group had arrived at the easternmost cliffs. Gulls circled overhead cautiously, the island's only form of native life. Gravis felt his gut wrench as he looked down and saw the half obscured waves crashing against the rocks beneath. They were high enough now that one wrong slip could prove fatal.

Still, Blessed tried to keep their spirits up. "So, Mr Teethsmasher, or may I call you Thorof?"

"First name's fine Blessed."

"Ah yes, the surname doesn't seem to suit you in all honestly. Take that as a compliment."

"I shall."

Gravis smiled. "Tell me. How does an Orc from a family of mercenaries come to have such a refined manner as yourself?"

Thorof was quiet for a few moments. Gravis assumed that Thorof wanted to remain secretive about his past. He was, after all, just as secretive. Despite this, he saw the Orc's large jaw hang low. Thorof didn't look obstructive. It was more in frustration. Thorof looked tired.

"Not yet," He said finally. "Now is not yet the time."

"Suit yourself," shot Blessed, a little insulted.

"Well how about you Mr DeMonfort?" Gravis said, deciding to diffuse the tension. "That's hardly a traditional dwarvern surname now is it?"

"No," Blessed laughed jovially, scaling a series of rocks. "No it is not. Would you believe that I have a little human blood in me?"

"It wouldn't surprise me." Gravis replied.

"Yes indeed. My great grandfather was a member of the Lyon nobility. Met my mother during the Industrial Revolution. She worked as an engineer you know? Was bringing the steam train to the mainland."

"I see."

"Of course, you, more than anyone else here should know what happened next Mr Grayslate. I do believe you would have lived through it"

A sly look ran across the Gravis' face. "I was but a boy back then, and we dark ones had our own problems."

"Oh indeed," Blessed laughed again. "But you need not worry Mr Grayslate. I harbour no such prejudices against your people, and neither I expect, does Thorof."

"None," the Orc said simply.

"Were most of the realms so open minded." said Gravis grimly. "In answer to your original question, yes, I recall the collapse of the continent's monarchies."

"My great grandfather was left with a choice; return to Lyon and remain forever exiled from his wife, or stay with her, forfeiting the chance to return to his lands and titles. In the end, he chose love over duty, and now nothing remains of him but the family name." He turned and sat on another rock. "And that is why, each generation, my more traditionally named dwarvern peers name us 'Blessed'."

Gravis smiled again. It was a good story, and he more than anyone else loved a good story. Thorof didn't seem to share his sentiment though, as again he was caught staring vacantly into the mists.

They didn't say anything for a few moments.

"And you, Mr Grayslate," Blessed said. "What answers do you seek on Castor island?"

Gravis turned and looked at the dwarf.

"I have my reasons Blessed. That is all you are permitted to know."

Blessed sighed. "Everyone is so enigmatic today. Very well, let us continue."

****

The three men made small talk as they scaled the west side of the island. It was a smooth incline, but it was not easy. The grassy patches soon cleared away until they were on nothing but a rocky path. The fog was getting denser, and it wasn't long until they could only make out the few feet ahead of them. The view of the sea was completely obscured.

Gravis regretted his choice of attire, but reminded himself that he hadn't gone through a day in his life without looking appropriately dashing, and he wasn't about to start now. He ran a hand through his wavy hair and felt sweat on his brow. Thorof and Blessed were out in front fading into the mist. If he slowed down there was a real possibility that they he might never find his way after them.

He strode on, pulling a hip flask out of his inside pocket. He took a swig of brandy. Not the wisest choice to be sure, but it made him feel better. A dark elf was never content unless he could enjoy himself at least once per day.

Over the last couple of hours Blessed's optimism had begun to wane. Thorof had remained as tight lipped and professional as always, but Blessed, having begun to complain about his joints, threw a few barbs at himself about getting old. Each laugh became more forced than the last.

After spending about an hour scaling the base of the mountain proper, Blessed decided it was time to rest up and prepare for dinner. Blessed pulled out a host of sandwiches made of thick bread, and a series of pork pies. He shared the provisions out amongst the other two. Gravis pulled a flask of smooth dark coffee from his pack. Just the smell of the beans as he opened it was enough to bring him to his senses.

"Amazonian," Thorof said, without looking over.

"That's right," Gravis nodded. He always bought the specific blend from a specialised seller when he could. "How could you tell?"

Thorof smiled, his massive under-bite surprisingly sly. "Call it a hunch."

Gravis took a sip of the dark liquid. There was something about Thorof he was unsure of.

****

They had scaled most of the mountain in silence. It was dark now. Cold. The three men huddled round a fire as they camped out in a small cubby hole in the rocks. Blessed had roasted rabbit for them, but despite the rest and the food, all three felt drained and demoralised. They made small talk as Blessed passed around the brandy.

"Forgive me if this is a personal question Gravis," he said as he poured out a cup. "How difficult do you find it being a dark elf?"

Gravis didn't say anything at first. He thought carefully on how to answer. "You ask that as though it could be summarised though one man's experiences."

"I wasn't implying that everyone of your race was the same," Blessed said defensively, waving his hands in the air. "I merely wanted to know what trials your day to day life entails."

Gravis took a swig of brandy and felt the warm liquid tear its way down his

"The three men made small talk as they scaled the west side of the island. It was a smooth incline, but it was not easy.."

throat. He'd rather not discuss his people's plight with outsiders. A days hike was hardly sufficient to earn a person's trust.

However, here and now, miles from civilisation, they might as well have been the only people in the realms left alive.

“It's not difficult, mostly. It's easy to hide who you are.” He looked down. “You're a dwarf Blessed, I imagine you worship your ancestors regularly.”

“I do,” he nodded. “Even the human ones.”

“And you have that...” he snapped his fingers. “Festival every year. Right?”

“The tribune, yes.”

Thorof's eyes flicked quickly between the two men.

“Well imagine all that culture, all your traditions, both grand and trivial. Imagine you couldn't partake in any of it, because the society around you deemed it unseemly.”

Blessed took a swig of the brandy and winced. “Well, I see what you mean, but the dwarven festivals don't tent to involve fooling around with anybody and everybody.”

Gravis rose to his feet in anger.

Blessed said, on the defensive again. “I wasn't implying... It just slipped out!”

“For the record, I haven't bedded man nor woman in decades.” Gravis' voice was calm, but it was building. “But the fact that you tell me you hold no such prejudices and then trivialise my people's culture to be about rutting like common animals is an insult I will not permit.”

Blessed smiled, tried to show that he wasn't intending to be cruel. It didn't work. Thorof remained seated.

“Our people's art goes further than you could possibly imagine dwarf. We understand beauty in ways other cultures only brush aside. We rebelled against an empire for what we believed in. We face persecution on a good day, and execution on a bad."

"Gravis, I meant no offence. Please, sit."

But Gravis didn't sit. His voice deepened, and his eyes glazed over. Blessed couldn't say for sure, but the fog itself could have grown darker.

"I have lived through centuries of unreconciled crimes against my people dwarf."

"Gravis calm down." Blessed said, unsure what else to do.

"Calm is a privilege I give far too readily," Gravis shouted. "I could kill you with a word!"

"But you won't," said Thorof. "You won't."

His voice was calm, yet commanding. Suddenly an equilibrium had settled across the camp. It were as though Gravis and Blessed's disagreement hadn't even happened.

Gravis, though calming down, was still ready for blood. "What do you know of what I will and won't do Orc?"

Thorof took a swig of tea from his cup. "Because you haven't before, and won't now."

"What do you know of me Orc? We've been together but a day."

Thorof put down the cup. "I know you better than you think Gravis. Sit down. It's time."

Gravis wasn't sure of where Thorof was going with this, but there was a gravity to his words that made Gravis forget his anger. He sat.

"This isn't the first time I've scaled Castor Island." Thorof said.

"You've done this before?" Blessed said, ecstatically. "Why didn't you tell me?"

Thorof looked up. "This isn't the first time I've scaled Castor Island with you either."

The two men were silent, trying to decipher what it was Thorof was trying to say. Finally Blessed broke it. "I don't understand."

"Gravis wasn't sure of where
Thorof was going with this, but there was a gravity to his words
that made Gravis forget his anger.
He sat."

"You wonder how an Orc can be as educated and gentlemanly as I? Truth be told I wasn't always this way. I was just like my brothers, a hired thug. One day a man came. You, Blessed. You needed two men to join you on your trip to Castor Island and you could only find one, so you hired an Orc that was too stupid to know what he was getting into."

"You approached me." Blessed said, practically a whisper.

"Because I grew tired of waiting," he took another swig of tea. "Let me finish."

The two men didn't interrupt again.

"So, one morning, looking for work, I was hired by Blessed DeMonfort to help him scale Castor Island with him and Gravis Grayslate. We did. We got to the top, to the ruins of the Aether's alter or whatever in the hells it is. And then, I'm gone." He tapped his hard skull for emphasis. "I'm back in my bed at home. It's the following morning, like nothing ever happened."

Blessed was about to interrupt, but then thought better of it.

"So I'm thinking it was all a dream, or I'd hit the drink and the drugs too much over the weekend. Weeks go by. A month maybe. Then Blessed DeMonfort comes to me again. Same deal, no memory of what went down. So I scale Castor Island with him and Gravis Grayslate. Again. It plays out identically. We get to the top, and I wake up in bed, the day after the last I remember. A few more months go by, and It happens again. And again. Sometimes only days separate it, sometimes years. But time and time again I keep waking up on the day we go to Castor Island."

It took a while for it to sink in. The realms were home to many fantastical things, of gods and monsters, but what Thorof was explaining was unreal.

"So what are you saying Thorof?" Gravis asked. "You're from the future and you keep getting taken back. Or are me and Blessed losing our minds?"

"I don't know," he said quickly. Clearly Gravis had asked this of him before.

"Every time I've asked, you seem to be up to current affairs. It's almost as if this day is sliding through history with me."

"So why do you come?" Blessed said, a fear in his voice. "Why don't you just stay away?"

"Because I need answers. Because I know, deep down, If I can only remember what I see at the summit, I'll know why I keep getting brought back here."

"How do I know this is true?" Gravis shot at him, accusingly. "How do I know you're not just making this up?"

"How would I know about Lileth otherwise Gravis?"

The elf's face dropped. It was as though he had been hit over the head with a rock. His eyes glazed over at first. Blessed wasn't sure of the significance of the name, but he could tell that it clearly meant a lot to Gravis.

"What do you know of Lileth?"

"I know you love her, but you are not *in love* with her. I know she is like family to you, yet you are not related. I know you'd give your life for her, though you hope it would never come to that. I know you're closer than lovers but you'd never be intimate with her, nor she you. I've been up this summit with you more times than I can remember Gravis. We've talked about your hopes and dreams, your fears, your follys, but the one thing I've never gotten out of you is what it is you hope to find at the summit of this mountain. I'm willing to bet it's got something to do with her."

Gravis didn't say anything. He nodded, clearly Thorof knew everything he needed to show Gravis solidarity. There must have been something between them for him to have opened up in this hypothetical past.

"Extraordinary," said Blessed. "Absolutely extraordinary. This must have something to do with the unique qualities of the island. I must write this down and record it for my book."

Gravis didn't say anything, just looked Thorof in the eyes and listened the sound of flags flapping in the wind.

****

The three men had risen early. Gravis and Blessed were a little unsure of what to make of Thorof's revelation. Scrutinise it though they did, it became abundantly clear that Thorof had an answer for every question. None of them could shed any light on the mystery.

Having expended their curiosity, the men completed the last leg of their journey in complete silence. Before long the difficult rocks began to level out, and a clearly designed path began to present itself before them.

The all encompassing fog began to dissipate. Grey and silver walls came into view. They were at the summit at last, with what appeared to be a large roofless theatre or alter awaiting them.

The structure had the characteristic design of all Aether ruins. The stone had a metallic sheen embellished with sly ridges of some glowing red mineral. The flags that had led them all the way to the top were tied round a series of poles. It was eerily silent, save for the flags.

"Incredible," said Blessed in awe. He immediately pulled out his journal and began sketching things down. Seconds later he ran over to what appeared to be some kind of balcony or viewpoint. "Ah yes. The theories could be correct. You can see straight down to the shoreline from here. Perfect if you wanted to watch a burial at sea."

Gravis wasn't here for a history lesson however, and he turned to see Thorof running his hand along the wall, trying to determine if it was metal or stone.

"Ringing any bells?" Gravis asked him.

"Nothing," said Thorof, making no effort to hide his disappointment.

Blessed was talking to himself still, rambling about the possible purposes of the structure. Gravis looked up, his eyes following the string of flags. They raised higher and higher, until Gravis's head had tilted vertically. The flags spiralled off into the mists above.

Suddenly something dawned on him. “What are the flags tied on to?” Gravis asked to nobody in particular.

The wind had picked up, drowning out his voice.

Blessed didn't seem to hear him, still thinking out loud and scribbling notes into his journal. There was a rabid intensity to his movements, not like Blessed at all.

Thorof by contrast was still tracing the wall with his hand. He had to shout over the sound of the wind. “What?” he called to Gravis.

“The flags.” Gravis shouted back. “What are they attached to? They just seem to get higher and higher. But there's no more support beams or poles or... well anything.”

Thorof shouted something indistinguishable. Gravis couldn't hear him over the wind. No, it wasn't the wind. It was something else. A low moaning drone, at first, accompanied by what sounded like singing, or screaming. It was hard to say. Gravis' eyes were locked into the foggy sky now, trying to stay on the spiral of flags.

He could hear Blessed, still talking, but it was more like babbling now. Thorof had fallen to the ground, though when and why, Gravis couldn't exactly be sure. All he cared about now was the sky, the flags. *Where were they going?*

The sky seemed to get lighter. The sounds grew louder, clearer.

“What are the flags tied on to?!” he shouted like a mantra. He couldn't even hear the sound of his own voice.

The fog began to part, and something, something beautiful and terrifying came towards him framed by the flags.

****

"Gravis' eyes were locked into the foggy sky now, trying to stay on the spiral of flags."

Thorof ached. It took him a moment to figure out where he was. He stared up at the ceiling, old yellow paint peeling off around the corners. He looked over at a beaten old side table. An empty hypo was sitting there.

He sighed. As he sat up the light of the morning had begun to sting his eyes. He could hear sounds from below. His siblings were arguing about something. He heard the crash of pots and pans. Whatever it was about, he didn't want to know.

Thorof stretched his muscular arms and began to rub his legs. They felt numb, as though he had walked miles last night. He glanced over at the hypo. *How much had he taken?* No more than usual.

Thorof got to his feet. He thought back to what he could remember from last night.

Suddenly he realised there was somebody else in the room. He squinted. They were hard to make out. It took him a moment to realise they weren't the only one.

He turned around. They were tall like elves, but their skin was black and red. The shade of red itself seemed familiar. And their faces were sharper, more alien. *How many of them were there?*

A slender hand gently touched Thorof's shoulder.

****

"Ahhgh!" Gravis screamed as he came to.

He was back on the sand, by the boat. He wasn't sure how long he'd been out cold. He craned his head back, trying to take things in. He could hear the gulls circling overhead. It was probably midday, but it was hard to tell with the ever prevalent fog.

As he got to his feet, Blessed came marching over, that warm fatherly smile back on his face.

"Ah," he said, clasping a hand around Gravis' waist. "You're back."

"What happened?" Gravis rubbed his eyes instinctively. It was odd but he felt no fatigue.

"Your guess is as good as mine," he laughed. "What do you remember?"

"I remember..." Gravis closed his eyes and thought, trying to piece together the last few days as though they were a fleeting dream. "I remember getting to the alter, or whatever it was. I remember you talking about how you could see down to the sea. Little else after that."

Blessed smiled and tapped his journal as he had done many times before. "Got a lot of stuff down, a good sketch too, but it quickly descends into meaningless gibberish. Still enough for the readers that's for sure."

Gravis looked around in confusion. "What time is it? How did we get down here?"

Blessed shrugged. "Couple of hours. There are few answers to be had on Castor Island it seems."

Suddenly Gravis realised that the Orc wasn't with them. "And Thorof?"

Blessed didn't say anything at first, the smile on his face had gone. He nodded towards the boat.

Gravis followed, and he could see the once proud Orc tied down, a vacant look in his eyes.

"I just hope he got whatever answers he sought," Blessed said sadly.

Gravis put a hand over his mouth. "What will you do with him?"

"Take him back to his family," Blessed said with regret in his voice. "If they won't have him then It'll be to the nearest institution I imagine."

The two men took stock for a moment. So much lost and so little achieved it would seem.

"Time to go then I suspect." Blessed said, and started to board their transport.

Gravis nodded and made ready to embark, when suddenly he felt a sharp pain in his side.

Something had found it's way into his inside waistcoat pocket.

He turned away from Blessed, and out came an intricately decorated cube. It was brassy in colour, and segmented as though it were some kind of puzzle.

“Are you alright there Gravis?” Blessed asked, concerned.

He quickly spirited the cube away and turned. “I'm fine. Shall we?”

Blessed nodded, and though the two made way to end their adventure, Gravis got the feeling that his journey was only just getting started.

The Modern Realms Almanac

Part One - History and Eras

The Ancient Era - Unknown

The Fall of the Aether

The Aether were an ancient civilisation that once ruled the realms. Very little is known about Aether civilisation, from their form of government to whether they ruled as a peaceable people or were warlike. It is also not known if they were a collection of races or founded around one. Neither is it known what gods they worshipped or what technology they used.

Only two things are known about the Aether. First is their architecture, as ruins are found all across the realms, strange metallic buildings with red affectations. The second is that they are the only civilisation to perfect teleportation. Waystones, gateways allowing instantaneous travel from one place to the other, still stand across The Old Realms

Nobody knows what happened to the Aether, only that by The Dark Age any record or trace of their culture was long gone. The only other civilisation known to have formed at this point are the Elven kingdoms, though they would not have left The Valley of Wonders until much later.

The Dark Age – 500 Years

This was an age of barbarians and despots. Few grand civilisations stood in this era, instead the realms were mostly populated by warring tribes. Only the most ancient of civilizations, the Dwarfs, the Xiuht and the Ptolemic Nubian's were organised into a stable society at this point.

This was a time of grand warriors and ancient vendettas. This was a time of evil wizards pursuing mighty powers. Demonic influence during this era was commonplace and it wasn't until towards the end of the era that outright worship of the virtuous gods was even considered. Might, strength and brutality was respected during this era, and most legends of mighty warriors were inspired outright from that fact.

The Golden Age – 300 Years

The Golden Age began when an unknown warrior named Arthur washed up on the shores of Avalon and proclaimed himself king. He united the tribes and led a conquering crusade onto the mainland. Thanks to an alliance with both the Dwarves and the Elves, Arthur managed to conquer nearly all of what would come to be known as The Old Realms.

Arthur's crusade set down the foundations for more civilized nations and those who were not brought to heel became more developed themselves as direct retaliation. This era also bore witness to The Dark Pact that created both Dark Elves and Vampires, as well as the beginning of the Kaizan invasion of the mainland and the travels of Al Fajah. This era saw the foundation of many churches, religious orders and academic institutions, as well as great migrations of races and peoples.

This was a time of great heroes and bloody conflict. It was a time of imprisoned princesses, dark prophecies and dragon slayers. Most of what the is know about magic was learned through trial and error in The Golden Age, and the actions and history of The Golden Age still shapes the politics of the modern Old Realms in

Particular.

The War of the 3000 Mages – 50 Years

In the final days of The Golden Age, The High Lodge of the Academy of Magic in Lyon saw a gathering of three thousand students from all across the realms. In secret these students had perfected the magical art of invulnerability to it's critical point, and they conspired to take the realms under their own control. They did so to replace old Feudal and Religious orders with a democratic council.

After a few surprise attacks to demonstrate their power, the 3000 Mages declared their intentions to the realms. At first the nations of the Old Realms saw little to fear beyond a small rebellion and underestimated the 3000 Mages. After several one sided victories many of the continent's royalty unconditionally surrendered to the Mages.

This did not clearly end the conflict however, and most of the continent's people broke loose from their royal allegiances. A continent wide resistance sprang up against the new order while the 3000 Mages spread their own spearhead south and east in an attempt to subdue the Golden Lands and the Dawn Realms. While their attention was elsewhere, the resistance secured an alliance with the Dwarven Empire and the Elven Kingdoms.

The most significant act of this era was The Battle of Everwinter. Here a great Elven army attempted to cut off and destroy the bulk of the Mage's forces as they headed south through the Everwinter Mountains into The Savage Lands. The battle was a massive defeat for the Elves and the sheer power of the magic clashing there led to a blast that levelled the continent's mountains, leaving behind a temperate bountiful landscape.

Victory for the Mages seemed assured, until hasty Dwarven research into gunpowder and the combustion engine gave the resistance the upper hand. Heavily industrialised transport distributed flintlock firearms across the realms at an alarming rate, and these weapons were too quick and too powerful for the Mage's invulnerability spells to counteract. The Mages were overthrown in a matter of weeks and the realms were free from their influence once more.

The Industrial Revolution. - 100 Years

After the falls of the Mages the realms were now free to rebuild. Due to their treachery during the war, most of The Old Realms' former royalty were executed by their people, and republics were formed. Only Lyon, Ruska and Wessex retained a monarchy. Trade began on a global scale due to the newly industrialised society and this is when The Golden Lands really started living up to their namesake.

What was formerly the Everwinter Mountains was colonised during this era. Naming itself 'New Dawn', the fertile land led to a quick succession of migrations and ultimately declared itself an independent nation. The other nations of the realms were too busy recovering from the war to assert any kind of claim, and New Dawn quickly allied itself with Pulotu and Moai to discourage any of those who would challenge it's independence.

During this time the Elven leadership of The Valley of Wonders entered a crisis. The common people wanted to capitalise upon the new technologies to cultivate the land through agriculture. The leadership disagreed, stating this would anger the Gods. This crisis led to a mass exile with only the loyal staying behind. A force field was projected around the valley and the High Elves isolated themselves permanently from the rest of the Realms, fearful of another conflict on the scale of the war with the Mages.

This was an era of change and adventure. An era of piracy, banditry and revolution. It saw technology progress at an alarming rate and diplomatic relations open up on an unprecedented scale. This was an era where the working man was empowered, where regimes were created and toppled almost yearly. This was a time when the industrialisation of war saw an end to the old ways and a start to the new.

The Modern Age – 50 Years and counting

The beginning of The Modern Age saw the realms changed in ways nobody saw coming. Long gone were the days of honour and personal codes. A cold war had begun between the remaining monarchies, now naming themselves The United Feudalist States, and the republics. The Kaizan war against the mainland was gaining full steam and political relations between the continents was getting more devious.

Dragon hunting, once a noble profession, now became a hobby for poachers. The dragon population dropped by seventy five percent and forced many concerned individuals to come together and form the paramilitary Draconic Preservation Society.

This era saw many rebellions in an attempt to return to the old ways, but all were ended brutally. Political manipulation, not military strategy, was the key to maintaining power now, and most alliances were formed out of convenience than any desire for the greater good. The Old Realms sit on the cusp of war, with the risk that the rest of the realms will be pulled in with it. Meanwhile The Valley of Wonders sits quiet and the Gods sit quiet with it.

The Modern Realms Almanac

Part Two – Nations

The Old Realms

The Republic of Avalon

Avalon is one of the oldest nations in the realms. The temperate island was once home to many warring kingdoms who were proficient in magic and had a strict honour system. In DA494 an aged man proclaiming himself to be king washed up on it's shores. Arthur, First King of Avalon, united the island and set forth on a crusade to conquer the mainland in DA500, kickstarting The Golden Age. Arthur left behind a chivalric code wherever he went, and his actions led to diplomatic agreement's with both the Elves and Dwarves.

In The Modern Age, Avalon's empire has long since receded, and it's monarchy was thrown out after The War of the 3000 Mages. However it is still one of the most influential nations in the realms. It was one of the founding members of ORTO (The Old Realms Treaty Organisation), and is an active participant in geopolitics.

The people of Avalon are openly accepting of racial diversity, but Arthur's chivalric code still persists, creating class and gender divisions that by right have no need to exist in a republic.

Henric

Henrick has been one of the most contested nations of the Old Realms. Mostly landlocked and forged from several kingdoms, the nation has undergone several civil wars. The most recent of which was against Feudalist separatists and there is still a nasty undercurrent of those still loyal to the former crown. Irrespective of this, Henrick has remained a strong nation economically and has strong ties to the Dwarven and Elven nations.

Florantino

A nation on the southern coast of the Old Realms, Florantino was one of the first kingdoms to spring up and attempt to claim an empire after Arthur's crusade. After conquering a modest part of the continent, the kingdom receded when it ultimately collapsed under it's own weight. The nation has been dealing with a struggling economy ever since, and the influence of Arthur's chivalric code would later manifest itself in the organised crime families that filled the vacuum of authority.

Bascilicata

A warm country on the far west of the continent. Bascilicata is so named for housing the headquarters of many of the realm's religious orders. Bascilicatan society itself does not mirror this piety however, and is rife with systematic corruption. Mostly untouched after the The War of the 3000 Mages, the Bascilicata government invested a great deal in Golden Land businesses. A popular retirement location for many film and music stars, the country is home to many billionaire playboys. Many such playboys use their gains to suck up to leaders and politicians of other nations in an attempt to further their influence

The United Feudalist States of the Old Realms

The UFSOR is a union of the last few states of the Old Realms that are still ruled under a monarchy and purport to practice feudalism (though the name is more ceremonial than anything else). The Union has had frosty relations with the rest of the Old Realms since the Industrial Revolution led to the execution of many royal families.

The Union sees itself as the last bastion of civilisation, and attempts to exert it's influence through clandestine operations and military action. However, the Union has long been in economic decline, and while what it lacks in resources it makes up for in numbers, any serious action would be doomed to failure.

Wessex

Wessex is the richest and most temperate of the Feudalist states. This nation began life as a bastion created by Arthur at the end of his crusade, and as a result Wessex has a lot socially in common with Avalon, even it's official language. Out of the three states Wessex has the most to lose, and is generally considered the voice of reason amongst the others.

Lyon

Lyon is the smallest but most wily of Feudaist states. It's people are flamboyant and big on ceremony. Lyon is the Feudalist nation that most attempts to ape the media expansion of the New Realms, and has had mixed results exporting it's own music and theatre.

Ruska

Ruska is the largest and poorest of the Feudalist states, encompassing mostly cold mountainous regions in the north. They are also the most aggressive of the states, having attempted invasion of neighbouring countries no less that three times over the last fifty years. It is said that Ruska rules not only it's own people through fear, but also the other Feudalist states, and that despite it's economic weakness, it holds the most influence in the UFSOR.

Tir

A warm island nation technically ruled by the government of Wessex, the people of Tir have been in open rebellion with their Wessex overlords for decades. The nation has many colourful festivals and traditions and is close to the religion of Urak. Many of Urak's followers belong to the Sons of Tir, a rebel group seeking to force Wessex control out of the isle through terrorist action. Wessex is not without it's sympathisers however, and the the island's otherwise pleasant climate has long been marred by the bloody conflict.

Teclovac

Teclovac is one of the neighbouring nations of the UFSOR and has seen several attempts, violent or otherwise, by the Union attempting to absorb it. Teclovac is seen as a stopgap against the Feudalists by ORTO and the rest of the Old Reams, and often gets assistance out of necessity more than friendship. Beyond it's political importance Teclovac has a strong artistic and architectural community, and it's aesthetic influence can be found all throughout the Old Realms. Despite danger from the Union, Teclovac often houses many expats from other nations who have come to study at it's artistic academies.

The Spirit Lands

Wendiga

Wendiga is the seat of the powerful Circle, and many outsiders incorrectly assume that they are the governing body. This is not the case, though there is some crossover. The Wendiga tribes formed a confederacy in GA76 and have persisted ever since. The power over earth magic granted by The Circle has resulted in most of the nation still being covered by a thick forest.

Wendigan's build their structures around the large trees, and live by an industry that takes no more from the land than it needs. The Wendigans have been slow to trust other nations, due to their past conflicts with the others on their continent as well as several broken treaties with Old Realms nations during The Golden Age and The Industrial Revolution.

Like most Spirit Land nations, the Wendiga practice gender neutrality, and a woman is just as likely grow to be a soldier as a man can grow to be a carer. The strict gender roles practised by other nations has led them to view the other realms with confusion.

Wonote

Wonote is an old rival of Wendiga and a started as a confederation of plains tribes. Wonotans come from a nomadic linage but were forced to create fortresses out of their rocky mountains during The War of the 3000 Mages. The great cities of the Wonote now stand upon these old fortresses. The plains are filled with natural resources. In recent years their abundance of crude oil has caused a diplomatic tug of war between nations in The Old Realms and The Golden Lands.

Sasgusaq

A humble nation in the frozen south. Sagusaq people live simple lives surviving the tundra with little interest in geopolitics. Igalutuk, their largest port city, is often the last port of call for those travelling to the Hellmouth, a well known fact that many Sasgusaqian's hate to advertise given their distaste and disinterest in the arcane world.

The Golden Lands

Vangaria

An old and powerful nation that once warred with Arthur's Crusade. The Vangarians still hold on to many of their military traditions and their Janissaries work as mercenaries for other nations, particularly the Feudalist Bloc. Vangaria was once a nation with close ties to the church of Urac but has long since been overthrown by the followers of Anima, which is it's dominant religion. Most of their cities are framed by great towers which Anima's priests sing prayers from every morning.

Nubia

A powerful desert nation once ruled by the Ptolemic Pharaohs but became a fully fledged republic long before the nations of The Old Realms. Nubia is nation covered in old tombs and is one of the few nations where Necromancy is permitted, with the Grand Necromancer holding a seat on the high council. Nubia saw many treasure hunters during The Golden Age and to this day aggressively seeks the return of many powerful artefacts currently possessed by other nations.

Amuntu

The most powerful nation in The Golden Realms and the one most responsible for it's namesake. Amuntu's government is much less significant than the corporations that it houses. The corporations are built upon the country's expansive gold mines and much of the nation's internal strife comes from it's unorthodox political structure. Coronet, god of commerce is a natural fit to it's people and magic sees little use outside of entertainment.

Al Fajah

The great flying city. During The Golden Age King Rahim sailed the city high over the skies of many a nation, travelling from place to place for his continued amusement. Several revolutions have taken place since the king's death and it is often said that the city is never far away from another. In it's current incarnation Anima is the dominant religion and the Imams maintain a choke hold on the ruling council, preventing them from any ideas on mobilising the city like in the days of old.

The Dawn Realms

The Kaizen Empire

A militant island empire that adheres to a strict honour code dictated by the Emperor and his Samurai lords. The Kaizen Empire has been at war with the neighbouring Khanates for as long as anyone can remember, to the point that it has been speculated it remains so due to it's government being unsustainable in a time of peace.

The Kaizen have had a great distrust in magic since the War of the 3000 Mages and in MA35 culled ninety five percent of the elven population due to their connection to the magical arts. This even was known as The Purges, and has left all but the most morally bankrupt of nations wanting nothing to do with the empire and it's affairs.

Yama

A nation of death worshippers and followers of Noctis. The inhabitants of Yama believe that the world, and both the heavens and hells, are part of a never ending cycle called 'The Wheel'. The people of Yama seek to free themselves from The Wheel, and are ideologically opposed to Necromancy and the Undead. Their cities are all built around great mausoleums, the grandest of which are reserved for their leaders. Most nations are neutral to Yama, they find their traditions morbid, but ultimately harmless on the political spectrum.

The Khanates of Buga

A loose collection of heavily armed tribes who have been at war with the Kaizen Empire for centuries. The Khanates are a simple people adept at agriculture and guerilla warfare. They have been kept armed and trained by many nations over the years in order to keep the Kaizens in check. The Khanates would otherwise not concern themselves with global affairs, but are constantly forced to get involved out of necessity.

Amazonia and The Savage Lands

Amazonia

A jungle nation populated entirely by women, the Amazons reproduce via a closely guarded earth magic ritual that takes place every year known as The Blooming. The Amazons have had a difficult history with the rest of the realms, and as a result are a very militant state. All Amazons are expected to serve in the country's republican guard at some point in their lives, and their warrior tradition is highly celebrated.

They have fought for and against nations in the Old Realms and currently distrust many of them due to the continent's male oriented bias. They are most closely allied with Wendiga, and face the most confrontation against the Kaizen

Empire, who have used Amazonia more than once as a staging ground without permission.

Houyhn

Sometimes known as The Beast Lands, Houyhn is home to many of the Realm's beast races, such as Centaurs, Nagas and Pegassi. It's most dominant resident, however, are a race of intelligent horses, who tend to day to day life in Houhn. The nation has little interaction outside of it's borders, as it's foundations of society seem so alien to the rest of the realms, and the feeling is pretty much mutual for Houyhn's populace.

The nation has strong links to the powers of magic, and often students of the arts will travel to Houyhn in an attempt to unravel it's mysteries. Few leave satisfied, however, but those that do often come out with an understanding of magic that transcends the material concerns of day to day life.

Xiuht

Land of the eastern dwarves. Xiuht is a dense jungle nation with ties to dark magic. The Western Dwarves once practised sacrifice in order to make deals with demonic powers for arcane knowledge. These deals still mark the nation today, with descendants hundreds of years down the line still trying to counter curses and ancient pacts.

The New Realms

New Dawn

Formerly the domain of the mountain dwelling frost giants, the Everwinter

Mountains were levelled during an intense battle between the Elven Kingdoms and the 3000 Mages. The land was reborn with bountiful resources and was soon settled by refugees after the war. Many kingdoms attempted to assert control over New Dawn, but as the war had left them in a weakened state the continent remained independent. In IR25 the republic was officially established.

Being a young nation New Dawn is seen as an inexperienced player on the international stage, but it's abundance of natural resources have caused it to grow quickly into a force to be reckoned with.

Other

Wati-Ku

The nations of the lizard men live in great glass bubbles under the Aeturnal Ocean, Wati-Ku is their only island colony and as such is their civilization's most predominant face to the surface world. Lizard Men are a harsh people, strong on "an eye for an eye" justice. Their society most predominantly worships Fataris, God of Justice and as such the lizard men are on good terms with many of the Knightly orders that still operate in the realms.

The Dwarven Empire

The Dwarven Empire consists of thousands of cities built underground all over the realms. While each city generally operates independently they are closely allied and any enemy movement against one would be considered an act of war against all. The Dwarves celebrate the Norðri Tribune every year at it's largest city Fyordug. The Tribune started as an alliance between the first three great kings but has since become a gathering for all of the first families to come together and reinforce the community that keeps the Empire together.

The Valley of Wonders

The first realm of the High Elves and home to Yggdrasil, the great ash tree that is the source of all magic. The Valley was home to the elves for hundreds of years and they never left until an agreement was made with Arthur during The Golden Age. Since then the elves have spread all across the realms but the Valley itself has refused to engage with any affairs outside it's own borders. This changed during the War of the 3000 mages and the elves sustained heavy losses.

The Industrial revolution lead to a crisis of leadership and seventy percent of the population were exiled by the ruling class. It was argued that industrialisation would anger the Gods, taking away all magic. Since then the nation's most powerful mages have projected a powerful barrier around the border, and none outside have heard from those within since.

Hellmouth

At the southernmost part of the planet is a gateway to the hells themselves. Hellmouth is a wretched hive that sits just on the outskirts. It is home to many demons who have left the hells due to angering their masters or making one bad deal too many. For mortals only the foolish or the desperate travel to Hellmouth, but it sees it's fair share in search of knowledge or power. The nations of the realms struggle to acknowledge Hellmouth's existence, though given that the vast majority of it's demonic population have travelled there to live in hiding that is probably for the best.

The Modern Realms Almanac

Part Three – Races and Creatures

Mortal Races

By the Modern era most races have spread out and mixed extensively across the realms. While some races retain a specific culture, most identify with the background in which they were raised. In Avalon, for example, a human, Dwarf and Elf, will all identify as Avalonians first. Likewise mixing of the races is very common with half elves and half dwarves being just as common as their full blooded contemporaries.

Humans

Most common of all the sentient races in the realms, humans are the most diverse in culture and appearance. They populate the realms from Avalon to Wendiga and are often make up the largest percentage of surface populations. Humans are typically seen by the other races as emotional and hot headed, often attributed to their relatively average lifespan in comparison to Elves and Dwarves. Humans have the most minimal racial identity, having sprung up from many different cultures over the course of the realm's history.

Elves

Originally descended from the High Elves of the Valley of Wonders, Elves are a race of tall slender beings of androgynous appearance and pointed ears. Elves have a strong affinity for magic and genuinely tend to have greater mental focus than other races, this gives them a reputation for arrogance and stuffiness. Most Elves tent to live about eight hundred years, though some make it as far as one thousand. This has led many Elves to take an active role in politics as their perception of time allows them to work towards a long game that most will never see in their lifetime.

Dark Elves

The Dark Elves are descended from a group of elves who took part in "The Dark Pact," an ancient ritual with the lords of hell that would give them power of Thanatos and Eros, death and sex. The price of this power saw the Dark Elves and their offspring forever marked with pale purple to almost grey skin. The Dark Elves were ostracised from society due to their reputation for hedonism and decadence. They still have to face many of these prejudices today. They hold on to their traditions tightly and in secret, though many have come out in the last few years calling for their ways to be respected and recognised.

Eastern Elves

It is unknown in what way, if any, the Eastern Elves are related to their western counterparts. While they share their slender frames and affinity for magic, they tend to only live a couple of hundred years. Their ears are much larger and point outwards while their noses are much smaller and rounded. The Eastern Elves have gone through many hardships over the last few decades, in particular the genocides inflicted upon them by The Kaizan Empire

Dwarves

The Dwarves are a stocky race who once lived predominantly underground. Dwarves tend to live about two hundred years but are an easygoing race with an affinity for conspicuous consumption. Their culture once celebrated martial prowess and a strict honour system but this has mostly died out in recent years, though all dwarves born of the first families are expected to attend the annual Norðri Tribune festival every year. Having worked as miners and blacksmiths in the past, Dwarves generally find themselves as captains of industry, running factories and fabricators more often than most.

Western Dwarves

A race of Dwarves separate from the cave dwellers. Eastern dwarves have hook like noses and large ears with tanned skin. They predominantly reside in the nation of Xiuht. They have a long history of meddling with ruinous powers and most families tend to come with some kind of curse or spiritual pact. This can sometimes have its benefits, with demons bound as powerful servants to a bloodline, but is looked upon suspiciously by others.

Halflings

Halflings are an easy-going race of rotund people just shorter than most dwarves. Halflings are labourers and have never had any particular ambition for power or politics. Halflings generally run things from an agricultural level, living in the rural areas of the realms and picking up and moving only if their way of life is threatened or a better piece of land presents itself. Halflings view most city folk with suspicion and rarely have time to consider the bigger picture. This is probably due to only living about forty years, most die of excessive eating.

Orcs

A race of tall muscular beings with rough features and tough green or yellow skin.

Orcs have spent most of history in periods of conflict, fighting as mercenaries with little sense of personal loyalty. This stereotype persists into modern times and most Orcs struggle to find work outside of soldiering and grunt work. Many Orcs resent this state of being but most attempts to rail against it have only led to violent outbursts that further reinforce these preconceptions.

Goblins

Like Orcs, Goblins have spent most of history in the employ of others. Mostly as spies and thieves in their case. Also like Orcs, Goblins too have been stigmatised as a result of this but unlike Orcs, Goblins rarely voice an objection to this status-quo.

Vampires

Another race that came about due to "The Dark Pact," Vampires are a race of humans turned into a creature of darkness by another Vampire. Vampires are the one race that is technically immortal though they are required to feed on blood to stave off ageing. This has led them to be treated as a threat by nearly all of the realms. Recently the Feudalist Bloc has offered asylum to any Vampires that would join their ranks. This is far from an act of charity however, as their invulnerability, ability to shape-shift and mystify their enemies has made them a great asset in the Feudalist's cold war against The Old Realms.

Lizard Men

A reptilian race from a civilisation beneath the ocean. Lizardmen are the most visually distinct of all the common races being reptilian rather than mammalian. Despite appearances Lizardmen have the most in common with humans than any other race, sharing their lifespan, drive and ambition. Unlike most other mortal races, Lizard Men cannot interbreed with the others.

Giants

Giants are an extremely rare race who primarily live out of the mountain regions of The Spine and what is left of Everwinter. They refuse to intermingle with the rest of society and are highly territorial. Most denizens of the realms do well to leave them alone.

Beast Races

Less of a single race and more a collection of races that can fit into a single classification. These include Pegassi, Unicorns, Centaurs, Sphinxes and other such creatures. Most have a high affinity for magic and co-ordinate only occasionally with the wider realms. Those that do tend to be experts in their field, diplomats or high ranking military personnel.

Elemental Born

Any member of the mortal races can be elementally born. What this means is that somewhere in their genetic bloodline is a connection to the elemental plane of fire, water, earth or air. This connection tends to manifest itself as a truly unique bodily trait. Some tend to be subtle like a blue hue to the skin or a fog over the eyes, others though can be very vivid such as green or blue skin, flames from the head or leaves in place of hair. Most elemental traits are hereditary and elemental born tend to have an affinity for the magic of their element type.

Despite their striking appearance, being an elemental born is seen as perfectly normal and studies suggest that at least twenty percent of the realms population has some form of elemental trait.

Immortal Races

The realms hold host to powers from beyond the dawn of time. Some of these beings derive their power from divine Gods, while others are creatures that descend from more primal origins. The realms often struggles to understand and accommodate these powers, though most are seen as being part of a system that mortal minds were never meant to comprehend.

Demons

Demons are manifestations of mortal emotions given flesh. They form from strong emotional occurrences within the hells and are psychically linked to all souls in the realms. They are a dark mirror to the emotions of mortals and generally seek to encourage greater emotions from those they were formed. Demons of greed drive people to further acts of selfishness, for example. The minds of Demons are difficult to understand, but those that spend prolonged time in the moral world begin to form feelings and personalities more in common with mortal minds. Some philosophers have speculated that demons are merely primal souls brought into being a different way to more common souls. Given the dangerous nature of demons, few have ventured to try and test this theory further.

Angels

Strange, one eyed creatures covered in feathers. Their voices are an unintelligible babble of whispers. Legend states that they are servants of the Gods, but the strange, seemingly random acts of the creatures has led many do doubt this in recent years. What is certain is that they are often seen fighting alongside paladins and priests of many faiths, and are sometimes seen taking the wounded or terminally ill directly into the heavens, body and all. Due to their unearthly nature, Angels are distrusted almost as much as demons.

Dragons

To the uneducated one may think that Dragons are little more than animals. Huge, nearly indestructible fire breathing animals, but animals nonetheless. In reality dragons are absurdly old, inhumanly intelligent creatures. Dragons do not perceive time the same way as mortal creatures do, this has made communicating with them very difficult. Dragons themselves have no interest in the affairs of mortals and often spend their time hoarding gold and staying out of the way. Their blood is often used as an illegal enhancement for magic users and as such dragons have found themselves pray to poachers armed with advanced weaponry. This has put many on the offensive in recent years, and efforts to open a line of communication with them has redoubled as a result.

Golems, Homunculli and Constructs

Creatures made of magic by powerful Wizards and Sorcerer. Most magical constructs lack a drive or independent thought but some of the most powerful magic users have been able to create artificial life in its own regard. These creations have never come into being without cost, however.

Spirit Creatures

Creatures neither of the heavens or hells, but of the neutral spirit world. Spirit creatures often come from the souls of forests, mountains or even the human heart. These creatures can be shapeshifters, dryads, fairies, old men of the forest and wisps. These creatures all follow their own code and are difficult to understand at times. They are simpler creatures than demons, often dedicated to a specific purpose, such as protecting the forest for example. For most, though, their purpose is never clear and dealing with them is an elaborate guessing game. For some cultures they are revered, while others see them as nothing but a nuisance.

The Old Realms Almanac
Part Four – Groups and Organisations

The Old Realms Treaty Organisation

ORTO is a union of nations formed in response to the aggressive activities of the Feudalist Bloc, but is more generally concerned with the well being of the continent as a whole. For practical purposes they act mostly as the military arm of the League of Nations and concern themselves with peacekeeping and relief efforts. They are not, however, above using clandestine tactics when they deem it necessary.

The Circle

More commonly, and incorrectly, refereed to as "The Circle of Druids." The Circle was founded by the very first folk to master Earth Magic and, as such, concern themselves with its teaching and regulations. They also act, to a degree, as the religious representation of The Earth Mother but rarely do they act as a church nor take any real pains to spread the faith. Instead they concentrate on enforcing the protection of the environment. They are particularly active on the political scene opposing heavy industrialisation.

The Dracomon

The Dracomon were once a a noble order of Dragon Slayers based predominantly out of the Kaizan islands. However, the tide of history heavily turned against them and currently they act as the dominant organised crime syndicate in The Dawn Realms. They are known for their focus on brute force over elegance and operate under a very strict personal code. Crossing the Dracomon is almost certainly fatal, but it is not unknown for one to negotiate a way out with a clear understanding of Dracomon culture.

The Draconic Prevention Society

With the onset of modern weaponry the once mighty Dragons found themselves endangered species in the face of poachers and treasure hunters. The DPS was formed by a group of concerned individuals in the name of protecting the Dragons. While they are an internationally recognised charitable organisation, the DPS often engage in brutal and questionable acts to meet their ends. They often rub up against law enforcement and military groups over questions of jurisdiction and have been accused of orchestrating terrorist acts against nations who choose not to recognise the group's legitimacy.

The 3000 Mages

The most powerful collection of magic users the realms had ever seen. The 3000 Mages were said to have perfected invulnerability, mind manipulation and immortality. At the end of The Golden Age they attempted a worldwide conquest that lasted fifty years. The Mages intended to reign over a society that disavowed hereditary inheritance and family ties. They planned to install a ruling council that would vote democratically on issues of state. Though long defeated, the influence of The 3000 Mages still hangs heavy over the realms. Members unaccounted for are still marked as wanted criminals by ORTO and many magic users style themselves in the image of the order.

The Elven Avengers

The most powerful and secretive order in Elven society. The Avengers were dedicated to the preservation of divine magic and strongly opposed to demonic influence and 'dark magics'. They primarily concern themselves with hunting down Dark Elves and Vampires. Kept alive by the most powerful magics, The Avengers, once noble warriors, are now withered husks dwelling in almost indestructible armour and driven by unstoppable rage. Their authority is not recognised by any modern nation and are seen as a nuisance by some and a dangerous threat by others.

Ayoade Global

Richest and most powerful out of all of The Golden Land's corporations, Ayoade Global has holdings and interests in nearly every developed nation. Known for it's ruthless business tactics and disregard for ethics in the face of profit, the corporation is nevertheless a strong progressive force in the realms. They continue to back regimes that resist the actions of the Feudalist Bloc and the Kaisan Empire and favour left leaning politicians. Provided they return the favour in kind, of course.

Paladin Orders

Paladins are the legacy of Knightly Orders that once recruited and fought across the realms in The Golden Age. Today they often serve as specialist military and law enforcement units. They favour no political affiliation but each chapter is generally loyal to the nation in which it operates out of.

The Order of Fataris

This order is probably one of the most active on a national scale, serving as special forces in military engagements. They often deploy from helicopter gunships, a throwback to when they once rode Griffons into battle. They are staunchly in favour of black and white morality and hate political wrangling behind the scenes. They are in particular opposed to the Feudalist Bloc, who's royal families they see as having escaped justice for giving in to The 3000 Mages over a century ago.

The Order of Urac

Members of this order are often found acting as first responders should a domestic incident fall beyond the expertise of common law enforcement. They pride themselves on only relying on lethal force when absolutely necessary and dress in bright white fatigues to to represent this ideal. They are viewed with suspicion by most police officers as they are rarely recruited from police ranks, and those officers that do find themselves chosen to join are referred to as "The Canonised."

The Order of Vox

Despite dedicating themselves to the God of War, The Order of Vox are rarely seen active in modern times. Mostly a ceremonial order now, they instead serve as a more social and political group. They recruit from combat veterans and often try to educate those who would seek violence for violences sake. There are a few chapters who still operate as a military unit, but they are often seen by the core order as a throwback to more barbaric times and try as best they can to disassociate themselves from these outliers.

About the Author

Jack Harvey has been writing for about as long as he can remember. With Twenty years worth of source material that means he's never out of ideas. While studying for a degree in English Literature and Media, he worked on a comedy sketch show and dabbled in stand up. Since graduating he's worked as a hospital radio DJ and won the annual Worlds Biggest Liar competition. Writing though, will always draw him back. He'll never stop telling stories, be they grounded, fantastical or dreamlike. You can read more of his work at eljackscomicsblog.blogspot.co.uk and contact him via email at el_presedente_nr@hotmail.co.uk

Jack lives in the north of England where he enjoys the solitude of the lonely mountains, but he also travels to the United States regularly. He was once told that he'd seen more of America than most Americans have. It's this experience of the wider world that heavily informs his writing, and he hopes it can truthfully reflect the diversity of the world around him.

65837580R00086

Made in the USA
Charleston, SC
05 January 2017